GÜERO-GÜERO:

THE WHITE MEXICAN

AND OTHER PUBLISHED AND UNPUBLISHED STORIES

Eliud Martínez

An Inlandia Institute Publication

INLANDIA
INSTITUTE

GÜERO-GÜERO: THE WHITE MEXICAN

AND OTHER PUBLISHED AND UNPUBLISHED STORIES

by

Eliud Martínez

2021

CONTENTS

All my work is dedicated to

The late Dr. Donald L. Weismann,
Professor Emeritus in the Arts, University of Texas, Austin

My dear wife Elisse and daughters Laura and Tanya

and

In memory of my mother and father

INTRODUCTION

I have had a longtime interest in my concept of "multiple ancestries" since I read the 1962 novel by the late Carlos Fuentes, *The Death of Artemio Cruz*. Ten days before Carlos Fuentes died, May 15, 2012, I presented, as a novelist and scholar, a scholarly essay at a conference held by Dr. Roberto Cantú at California State University, Los Angeles.

It was the second of two essays that focused on Mexico as "a thousand countries with a single name," a thought that occurs to the dying Artemio Cruz and which the novel dramatically illustrates with *criollo*, *mestizo*, *mulatto*, African and other characters from many historical periods that converge on Mexico. This essay was published on the 50th anniversary of the novel by Cambridge Book Publications in January 2015, in a book called "The Reptant Eagle" edited by Dr. Roberto Cantú.

I have also edited an anthology of student writing for which I have written a lengthy introduction where I had the opportunity to say that universities are now places of multiple ancestries. A lengthy introduction, consequently, is not necessary for this book. Many of the stories are based on the diversity that now is quite apparent in universities and in publications.

I did have the opportunity to present a paper on the subject of multiple ancestries in Dallas, Texas, at the 2009 annual meeting of HOGAR (Hispanic Organization for Genealogy and Research), subsequently published in an expanded version as "Mexico's Multiple Ancestries: Controversies in the Writing and Rewriting of Mexican

History," HOGAR, Vol. XIII, 2010, pp. 37-42. My conclusion is stated clearly: "Based on our multiple ancestries we should aspire to be—indeed we are—citizens of the world. World civilization and universal learning are ours to take, according to our individual desires, capacities and intelligence."

The stories that follow are also based on the premise that we are all citizens of the world. Some are based on real events and some have been thoroughly researched, some have never been published before, some have and they are reprinted with permission. The original sources are indicated in the acknowledgments. My hope is that all readers will find the stories enjoyable.

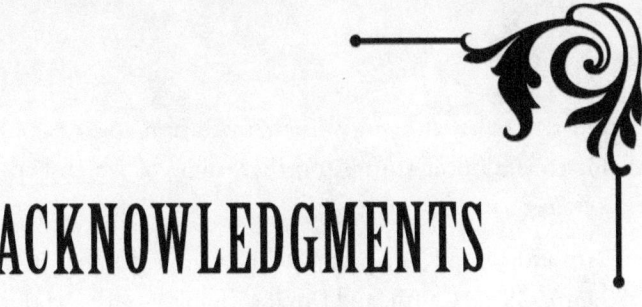

ACKNOWLEDGMENTS

T he author of these stories wishes to acknowledge grants to support research and creative activity from the UC Riverside Academic Committee on Research, and I especially wish to thank Dr. Arturo Gómez-Pompa, then the Director of UC-MEXUS, the University of California Institute for Mexico and the United States, and Kathy Vincent, (then) co-director of UC-MEXUS.

The author is also indebted to a wonderful storyteller, the late Sra. Guadalupe González De Loza, for two of the stories included in this volume, previously published; to Richard Romero, for his well-written and researched Master's thesis, "Eliud Martínez's *Voice-Haunted Journey*: The American Dream and the Political Unconscious," (Dept. of English, Cal State Los Angeles, 1996) which knowledgeably examines countless international influences at work on my novel. I wish to express special gratitude to Dr. Roberto Cantú—Professor at California State University, Los Angeles, an outstanding literary historian and critic of Chicano, Latin American and Comparative Literature and author of the essay, "Eliud Martínez" in the *Dictionary of Literary Biography, Chicano Writers II* (vol. 128), for his continuous encouragement, his customary insightful reading of my literary works and essays, and for his constructive criticism.

I also wish to thank the following persons at the University of Wisconsin, Stout: Professor Emeritus Rob Price, artist; Dr. Jean-Marie DuPlaise, the Department of English and Philosophy; Sharon Becker and the Multicultural Center staff; and the Department of Art and Design for inviting me in April 2006 to give a reading of my fictional works and to make a public presentation on the topic of Mexican film and cultural history. Their invitation coaxed me into bringing this collection of stories together, some of which had been written years ago.

In addition, I am grateful to Sulema Ramos, Jo Ann Valentín Cantú, Gloria Cantú, and Dorena Thomas—all of whom are members of *HOGAR de Dallas*—for the opportunity to present in 2009 from this collection of stories and one essay on Mexico. One story, "We Did Not Choose Our Fathers," and the essay "Mexico's Multiple Ancestries" were published in HOGAR in 2010.

Finally, I am very fortunate to come from a family of storytellers, to all of whom I am deeply indebted: my father Estroberto, my mother María née Correa, my sister Belia, and my brothers Estroberto, Jr., Heriberto, Adán, and my late brother Teodoro, Belia's fraternal twin.

My brother Estroberto, Jr. deserves special thanks. He is a person with an extra-ordinary memory. He is also a very generous person, and I am deeply grateful for his Virgilian assistance in keeping up with changes in Austin, Texas. For many years I stayed at his and his wife Lupita's home, and he has driven me everywhere to see with my own eyes the changes that have taken place in Austin, Texas. He has frequently kept me up-to-date on the Mexican community of Austin by telephone and by sending clippings from the local newspaper.

My sister-in-law Lupita is also a storyteller, and so are her daughters, especially Hopie (Esperanza) and the master photographer Diana. My brother Adán is like don Lucas in *Al filo del agua* by Agustín Yáñez, the keeper of obituaries of people of our generation. Usually he attends their funerals on our behalf, and he too shares his memories of the departed.

My sister Belia, whose intelligence, memory and storytelling abilities far exceed my own, is the keeper of our family history. With the help of storyteller husband Abelardo González she looked after her brother-in-law Ricardo who died of cancer at a young age. She and

Abelardo took care of her father-in-law in his old age, and my father too. Their stories of the last six years of our father's life greatly enrich many family stories. My father paid tribute to her by saying that "she knows how to look after old people."

And I am indebted to my dear wife Elisse for her assistance in compiling these stories, and to my daughters, Laura and Tanya, all of whom provided endless inspiration

The following stories were previously published: "Aunt Serafina" and "A Funeral in Guadalajara, Mexico" as "Two Norteño Short Stories," in *Mexican Studies / Estudios Mexicanos* (Vol. 12, No. 2, 1996; "Güero-Güero," in (*untitled*) vol. ii, issue ii, 1991: and "Aunt Serafina" as "La Tía Serafina," published separately, in (*untitled*), vol iii, issue i-ii, summer-fall 1997 and also in a shorter version in the (*untitled*) volume iii, Summer 1997, edited by Richard Romero, Antonio Roque and G. Guttierrez. This story was dedicated to my Corsican carnal, Roberto Cantú. Stories are re-published with permission. "The World of Dolores Velásquez," in *Grow Old Along With Me: The Best Is Yet to Be*, was published and edited by Sandra Haldeman Martz, Watsonville, California: Papier Maché Press, 1986.

I

BECKY'S PIANO RECITAL: "THE STORM"

Twelve years old, Becky is rehearsing at home for a piano recital. Her father Miguel is the audience. In the living room, pretending that she is on stage, she is standing a little distance away from the piano. Following her piano teacher's instructions, she is standing somewhat at military attention, in a formal and solemn manner, her arms held closely against her body. Becky is not supposed to smile when her turn comes up.

—Guy, Dad, she exclaims abruptly. The piano teacher told us not to smile or say "hi." We're supposed to look serious and composed, the teacher said. She told us to walk slowly to the piano and introduce ourselves and tell the name of the composition we will play and the name of the composer. "Speak slowly and clearly," she said, like you always say, Dad. I wanted to say "hi," but the piano teacher doesn't want us to.

The child is customarily playful and cheerful. Being serious goes against her propensity to laugh and smile. She stands stiffly with a serious look on her face. Now she walks glumly toward the piano, resumes her solemn stance, at attention. Without smiling she speaks. Her words are enunciated slowly and distinctly, and this pleases her father immensely. She sounds her g sharply, as her father has told her and Sara, her sister, since they were very little. Always sound your g's. Goin-g-g-g! Doin-g-g-g!

—My name is Becky Velásquez and I am going to play .... The child pauses. She is in a playful frame of mind. She smiles. There is laughter in her heart and childlike defiance in her spirit. Her father is deeply touched by his child, his precious little girl. *Hijita, mi corazón.* Becky starts over.

—Hi! She smiles with cheerful willfulness. Bending her body over to the side a little, she waves a little flag and says, My name is Becky Velásquez, and I am going to play a composition called "The Storm," by the world famous composer, Rebecca Velásquez.

For the rest of his life her father will remember proudly the composition that Becky is about to play, which is her very own and not the one which she will play at the recital for which she is supposed to be rehearsing. Becky and her father break into laughter.

Now Becky sits at the piano to play the composition which she composed a year ago. Her father was always touched and pleased whenever she played "The Storm." His daughter's composition always raised his spirits. He was so proud of his little girl, of the artist in her that he had seen emerging in her childhood, the artist that he was convinced she would become, of one kind or another. He was astonished at how much she knew about writing and music at her age. His heart swelled with pride whenever she discussed literature or music with him. Becky amazed him with her commentaries about characterization and themes in literary works. She had read some of her father's writings too, and she had made insightful, valid comments about his tendency to be repetitious, about character development, and more. Yes, he often thought proudly, she is already well on her way to becoming an artist. And she is only twelve years old.

Becky's father was pleased that some of her teachers, a few special ones, had the sensitivity to recognize Becky's talents, the quality of her imagination and creative abilities. How unfortunate when talented and gifted children go unrecognized by mediocre teachers, or by school officials like the principal of her elementary school. This woman, with her impeccably styled, dyed blonde hair, her cold and unfeeling, business-like manner, her artificial enthusiasm, and her need for dogmatic rules and administrative policies that had to be followed to the letter, allowed no exceptions. She had no sensitivity for specially gifted students and their artistic talents and creative gifts. Becky's father thought that his little girl's future would be in literature and the arts.

His experience had taught him that artists do not fit into neat categories, especially those defined by unthinking educators who worship cold numerical data and statistics, who employ so-called objective quantification methods of analysis and scientific instruments to develop rigid theories and paradigms and innovative educational models. Becky's father lamented that educators of this kind are incapable of appreciating and understanding gifted children. They cannot measure the quality of children's dreams and daydreams. They cannot recognize the radiant glow of inspiration when it brightens a child's face or the quick intuitive knowledge that children have from a very early age.

Becky was laughing with her father now. She was waving her arms dramatically, speaking playfully, and her father was deeply moved. His tenderness toward his little girl was boundless. He knew that his baby, as an artist, would be hurt from time to time. She would know sorrow and solitude. He wanted her to learn that self-knowledge comes from solitude, that laughter and playfulness count as much as seriousness, that gentleness is a source of abiding strength, that one must be able to stand on one's own feet, independently, and with others. He did not wish her to be solitary, nor to be dependent excessively on anyone else.

Her whole life was ahead, and she would be misunderstood. His whole heart went out to her. She was his flesh and blood, and he thought of how he had once regretted not having a son, mistakenly it now turned out, because he was so proud of Becky and Sara. He felt the closeness of their blood and his, and he cherished the bonds of art that they also shared with their father. He had romantic notions, as people who knew him well understood. Becky and Sara, like their father, he loved to think, were obeying the mystical calling of ancestral blood. Art was somehow part of their inheritance, which the girls' mother also praised and encouraged. He had given them diaries to keep not long after they learned to read and write. He and Natalie had instilled in them a love of reading too.

—When I am playing the piano, Dad .... Becky is beginning to explain her composition. He loved the way that she said, "Dad." She continued. I want you to picture in your mind the clouds. This is what I want you to picture first .... The child was using her arms to dramatize her words in a way that she knew the piano teacher would disapprove of .... First, the clouds moving across the sky, you know ... and she began to wave her arms when she said ... and the wind ... waving her arms to suggest the movement of the wind, slowly at first, then gradually faster and faster .... Imagine, Dad, the thunder, rolling across the sky ... and Becky made throaty sounds to suggest thunder ... and now the wind, no, wait, the rain comes before, you can hear it on the windows, at first it is soft, then it gets louder, building up to a storm, louder and louder, and towards the end, when the storm goes away, the music becomes soft again.

Little Becky took her seat at the piano. She is about to begin playing. She gives some instructions to her father.

—Now, Dad, when I say something, repeat what I say, okay?

—Very well, *hijita preciosa*, my honey.

—Wind, Becky says, as her fingers pass slowly across the keys of the piano.

—Wind, he repeats, imagining the wind passing softly through the trees.

—Raindrops, Becky says, as she touches some of the high keys a little faster to simulate drops of rain on the windowpanes.

Becky's father is spellbound by Becky's poise, the movement of her little fingers across the keys, by the artistic composition and by the piano's ability to conjure up images of an approaching storm. He is listening with untold pleasure and pride.

—Raindrops, Becky says, slightly annoyed because, being so enraptured, her father has not repeated the word.

She breaks the spell that the piano has cast over her father. There is a tone of annoyance in the word that she repeats again, firmly.

—Raindrops, he says at last.

The great pianist is impatient and disappointed in her father. Why can't he follow her simple directions?

—You said it too late, Dad. I don't want to do it anymore.

—Please Becky! I was just loving it so much. Please continue, m'hijita, mi corazón. He pleads. You were doing so beautifully, hijita, he says with a little sadness in his voice. Don't be impatient with me, please.

—No, I don't want to play the piano anymore, she says peremptorily.

After more pleading from her father, however, she begins to play again. Her father's eyes are radiant with joy and pride, following the movements of little fingers across the keys. Those of the left hand are producing soft low sounds on the piano keys. The right hand is doing something else. Gradually Becky's fingers begin to speed up, to run across the piano keys, her left hand moves across the low keys while the right hand produces other sounds on the high keys. The fingers of both hands now are moving quickly, in harmony with each other. Becky is inspired. Her little fingers produce soft sounds that become staccato and the musical composition moves into a crescendo.

—It's a very easy composition, Dad.

To Becky it is simple. Her father, however, is awed. He marvels at her composition and her playing. For him there is something elegant in the sounds. The composition has tapped some emotional mainspring of the child. For him there is magic in the creative gift that permitted Becky to compose music that captures and recreates the sounds of natural elements and forces.

The twelve-year-old child had composed the music the year before! She had heard the soft patter of rain upon a windowpane growing louder, of winds and storms increasing in force. There was something romantic about the staccato sounds and the crescendo. He wished that he knew something about musical forms. The repetition of the high keys produces delight in his heart, even though he does not understand what the right hand is doing on those keys.

Becky is playing her own composition with genuine and enthusiastic inspiration. In her father's eyes she is radiant at that moment. He can see and hear the soft wind passing through trees, the gathering of dark rain clouds, the patter of rain drops upon the windowpanes, the beginning of the storm, the rain falling harder and harder, and the rolling of thunder across the dark-clouded sky, becoming louder and louder. There is the storm now, in all its force. It lasts for just a few moments. Now Becky's fingers slow down, gradually. Her left hand moves back to the low keys. Her right hand, too, moves towards the lower keys. The composition moves into a diminuendo. The storm begins to recede, slowly, ever so slowly.

Finally, the composition is over and Becky's father applauds with all his enthusiasm. *Hijita*, oh my baby! I love you with all my heart. I am so proud. A single pair of hands is clapping loudly, warmly. Becky thinks her father is such a silly man to be so enthusiastic about something that is so simple, so easy to play.

The private recital of Becky's composition is over. Her father expresses curiosity about the technical aspects. He asks Becky to explain the keys. He asks her why she says the composition is easy.

—The left hand only plays two chords, Dad. Most compositions have a lot of chords. The left hand only plays C and G, C-G. And the right hand plays C-D-E-D-C.

She goes over the parts of the composition one by one and demonstrates them on the piano. She demonstrates that she has simply used the same simple movements over and over, with variations.

When Becky has explained the entire composition, her father does not really understand, but he is fascinated by her systematic craft-consciousness. In her explanation she points out how each part relates to the others, and she uses language that her father does not understand. Nevertheless, she senses her father's admiration and pride. He really appreciates her composition. She has made him very happy. In her mind his praise is extravagant for such a simple thing. Poor Dad. He doesn't know anything about piano or music. He asks so many questions. The child is pleasantly amused by her father's curiosity and because she knows that no matter how many times she might explain "The Storm," her father will never understand.

Becky, my sweetheart, *mi corazoncito*. You are growing up, my honey. I love you with all my heart.

In years to come he will not be able to convince Becky that in his judgment, "The Storm" is a masterful artistic composition by an eleven year old. Her father hopes, even so, that she will never forget that their hearts met at that private recital which he would cherish to the end of his life. One day, my honey, my enthusiasm will make sense.

II

AUNT SERAFINA

A *NORTEÑO* LOVE STORY

The old man, head bowed, was standing next to his son Miguel, over the grave of his other son Alejandro at the Mexican cemetery in Pflugerville, Texas. There, at the west edge of town, both men, a father and a brother to the dead man, were paying their respects, in silence. Nearly eight years had passed since Alejandro had died. From the near distance came the sound of heavy traffic on the I-35.

Since childhood, walking through a cemetery and listening to the humming of automobile tires on asphalt roads always turned the younger man into a daydreamer. For him it was like listening to an afternoon symphony. He glanced up at the great sky of Texas. He was home again, and he remembered other sounds from his childhood in the country—of roosters crowing in the morning, cows lowing, hens cackling, pigs grunting, and horses neighing. He remembered the shrill thrilling songs of *chicharras* in summertime, the buzzing of flies and mosquitos, and dogs barking. The recollection of these sounds made his entire childhood pass across his memory. Now too, the cemetery made him contemplative. This cemetery must be full of stories, he said when he and his father were remembering Alejandro. With his gaze still turned upward his father inhaled deeply. Here, at this Mexican cemetery, in a town settled by Heinrich Pfluger and his family in 1846, Miguel Velásquez pondered the cemetery's power to conjure up strange and wonderful stories of the human heart and its irrepressible propensities.

His father raised his gaze away from his son Alejandro's grave, and he looked out across the cemetery. His strong fine nose lifted, he squinted his light brown, almost hazel eyes slightly, perhaps to correct his old age vision. Despite his being in his eighties he looked like a man in his sixties, and he did not wear glasses. He was looking slowly from one side to the other as if to get his bearings. Then the old man raised his arm and pointed to a grave not too far away. *Mira, hijo,* he said. The son spoke only Spanish with his father.

—Look, hijo, over there is Leopoldo Cantú's grave. Seeing the name in large letters on the headstone reminds me that he told me a story once, about his aunt. What was her name? It will come back to me in a minute. You are right when you say there are many stories buried with the Mexican people in this cemetery, hijo ... *sí,* now I remember. Her name was Serafina. One day several of us were going to play poker at Leopoldo's house. I was the first to arrive, and I started looking at some old photographs on top of a dresser. Leopoldo came over when he saw me standing in front of a picture of several people. He told me who they were, and then he told me the story of his aunt Serafina.

This little girl in the picture is my *tía* Serafina, Leopoldo said, when she was ten years old. Next to her is her father, my grandfather Arturo. The boy in this picture is my father Dionisio. He was twelve years old. The other two girls are my father's other sisters, Imelda, eleven, and Cristina, nine years old. And the man you see standing next to my grandfather is his best friend and compadre, José Franco. The two men and their families were neighbors. They raised cattle, and their ranches were close by.

Leopoldo took the picture from the top of the dresser and held it in his hands. He shook his head like a person does who looks back to the past, knowing what is going to happen in the future. Then he did in fact tell me about what happened to his *tía* Serafina four years later.

Four years after this picture was taken, when my tía Serafina was fourteen years old, José Franco fell in love with her.
They say that she fell in love with him too. She knew that José
was married, that he had a family, and on top of that he was
nearly three times her age. She went off with him anyway. He
was the best friend of tía Serafina's father, Arturo Cantú, my
grandfather. My grandfather found out somehow that his compadre José was about to run off with my tía Serafina. Being best
friends and compadres did not stop José: he wanted tía Serafina so much that he killed my grandfather. This happened in
a small town back in Mexico, near Guadalajara, and when my
tía ran off with José Franco, well of course this created a big
scandal in the town. Yes, they ran off and he left his family. My
grandmother Nieves was very hurt. How could Serafina run off,
she asked, with the man who killed her own father? From now
on I never want her name mentioned in this house ever again.
I never had this daughter. From now on she does not exist, my
grandmother said.

José had his way with my tía for a few months. Then he tired
of her. One day he left her in a house of prostitution and went
back to his wife and family. Not long after, he found out somehow that tía was going to have a baby. Based on how long ago
he had left her at that place José figured it had to be his baby.
Bueno pués he took her out of there until after she had the baby.
It was a boy. Then he took her back to the same place, left her
there again, and took the child. José Franco threatened tía Serafina: if she ever came looking for the boy he would kill her. I
killed your father, he told her, and he was my best friend and
compadre. You are nothing to me. I will kill you if you ever
come after the boy. Do you hear?

José Franco took the child and went back to his own family. He raised the boy having him believe that José's wife was

his mother and that the older children were his brothers and sisters. He threatened them too. They did not dare tell the boy the truth while José Franco was alive. The little boy was José Franco's favorite. He adored the boy more than any of his other children. When José died he left everything to the boy who was now in his twenties. All this time José Franco's family hated the boy.

Meanwhile, tía Serafina was very lucky, because not long after she had the baby, when she was in that place, she met a man who was very, very good to her. One of my other aunts got to know him many years later, and she said that he was a wonderful and understanding man. He had to pay two hundred pesos to get her out of that place. That was a lot of money in those days. He was a wealthy man. He married her and took her to live in Mexico City. But she never forgot her son. She of course remembered José Franco's threat that he would kill her if she went looking for the boy. So she didn't.

After José Franco died and left everything to the boy, Franco's wife had nothing to be afraid of, so she told the boy, whose name was the same as his father's, that he was not her son. His half brothers and sisters hated him, had always resented him, because he was the father's favorite. The father's corpse was still warm when she told him.

—You are a bastard, José. I have hated you all these years, since your father brought you here. I am not your mother.

Pués, if she was not his mother, he wanted to know who his mother was.

—Who then, he asked, is my mother?

And José Franco's wife told him to go ask that Cantú woman who runs the little cantina in town.

—She is your grandmother. Your mother is her daughter Serafina. She was no good. Fourteen years old and running off with a married man so much older than her, who killed her father, how disgusting!

And she probably called her a few other names.

José Franco's wife and her sons hated the young José even more, of course, because José Franco left him all the money. Anyway, the young man went to town and stopped at the little cantina. He took a table, and when my grandmother Nieves came to serve him he introduced himself. He said that his name was José Franco, like his father.

—My father died only a few days ago, he said.

And my grandmother told him that although she was sorry that he lost his father, and she expressed condolences, she asked that he please not mention his name in her presence.

—Now, what may I serve you, *joven*?

He ordered a tequila. Maybe it would calm his nerves after getting the surprising news from José Franco's wife.

—I understand that my real mother is your daughter Serafina.

—I have no daughter by that name, my grandmother said to my cousin.

He was my cousin you see, her grandson, *como yo*. He was flesh of her flesh that she would not recognize. Her grudge did not permit her. She had made a vow never to forgive my tía Serafina. For my grandmother my tía Serafina did not exist. And to this day I do not know what feelings, if any, she had toward this grandson. He was not to blame for the way that he came into the world.

Life is strange, the octogenarian commented. There are

things that are difficult to explain, but they happen. Anyway, I am getting ahead of the story, he said. Leopoldo told me more.

—Somehow, Leopoldo said, the news reached my tía Serafina in Mexico City that José Franco was dead. There is a rumor that my tía Imelda stayed in touch with her sister secretly, without my grandmother's knowledge. She may have told her. One day tía Serafina came back to the town to look for her son. He was now about twenty-five or twenty-six years old. After he was born my tía never saw him again. They say that she came to my grandmother's house when she was away, working at the cantina. My tía Imelda said that tía Serafina was very well dressed and that she was wearing a hat. People who saw her say that she looked very elegant, like a rich woman. Yes, the man that she married was wealthy. My aunt Imelda broke down and cried when she saw her sister. She could not let her sister in the house, however, because of my grandmother. Standing at the door they hugged and cried together, and tía Imelda agreed to help bring tía Serafina and her son José together.

—But Mamá must not know, tía Imelda told her.

Also, my cousin found out after José Franco died that his mother lived in Mexico City. I guess tía Imelda told him. How in the world, he must have wondered, could he find her there? It would be useless to go and try to find her in a city larger than Guadalajara. He thought of his mother often.

Later, on the same day when tía Serafina came to the ranch, my tía Imelda talked to José and told him that his mother was looking for him. By that time tía Serafina, having given up hope of seeing her son, had gone to take the eleven o'clock morning train back to Mexico City. Knowing that the people of the town never forgot the terrible scandal of many years ago, she could not bring herself to stay.

Now, upon hearing that his mother had come looking for him, and that she had taken the morning train back, José decided to take the one o'clock afternoon train to Mexico City. He did not even know her address. Or maybe my tía Serafina gave it to tía Imelda, and she gave it to him. I don't know.

Two strange coincidences happened that day. First, they both were there but missed each other at grandmother Nieves' house by one or two hours only. The second coincidence was that my tía Serafina had missed the earlier train. Without knowing it, she and her son were on the same one o'clock afternoon train going to Mexico City from Guadalajara. In the same compartment! Can you imagine that, Antonio? How strange is life, ¿verdad hombre? Bueno pués, she noticed the young man who looked very much like José Franco. Tía Serafina got up from her seat, went and sat next to the young man. I heard two different versions of what happened on the train. But what matters is that mother and son, who had not seen each other since he was born, were indeed on the same train. This is the version that makes more sense to me.

—Please excuse me for asking, young man, she said. Are you from these parts?

—I found out recently that I was born in Chihuahua, he said. But I have been living in a town near Guadalajara since I was a child.

—Will you permit me to ask about your mother?

—She lives in Mexico City. I do not know her. My tía Imelda told me that my father took me away from her right after I was born. She is my mother's sister, my aunt, and she told me that she came looking for me today, but we missed each other at my grandmother's ranch.

Now my tía Serafina knew, but she had to know if her son

had been told anything bad about her.

—And did your father tell you about your mother?

—No, until he died I always thought that the woman who raised me was my mother. She is the one who told me who my real mother is.

—And what is your name, young man?

—*Me llamo José Franco, como mi* padre.

—*¡Ay, hijo!* I knew it when I saw you. I am your mother.

Miguel's father paused for a moment, took a deep breath, and shook his head in disbelief. In telling Leopoldo Cantú's story the old man had completely taken over the character of the man over whose grave he and his son were now standing, and indeed of the people in Leopoldo's family.

Miguel looked again at the grave stone. Yes, he thought, letting his eyes wander across the entire cemetery, each one of these Mexican people buried here has a story. Each person was part of a family. They loved and suffered, toiled and rested. Ordinary Mexican people, whom we were once accustomed to think of as simple and negligible, had brought many children into the world. The history of Pflugerville does not take these Mexicans into account. It only tells about the people buried at the other part of town, people of German ancestry, in the cemetery next to the Immanuel Lutheran Church. It seemed strange at that moment, to think that many of the novelists, poets, painters, dramatists, musical composers, and painters whom he truly admired were German.

But for his father's extraordinary storytelling he might have let his mind wander among the arts of Germany. Instead, pondering the amazing love story that Leopoldo Cantú had told his father, and that his father had just shared with him, he became keenly conscious of being presently under the large Texas sky. He was moved by the story in such a way that he experienced an exhilarating sense of the mystery of life. A sense of the immensity of the territory that once belonged to the country of his ancestry added to his exhilaration. He had listened carefully to his father's storytelling. Now Miguel spoke.

—And is there more to the story, Papá?

—Well, about the time that Leopoldo got to this part of the story the others who were going to play poker with us started arriving. Leopoldo told me that after meeting his mother on the train the young José Franco went to live with her. He lived with his mother for a little over a year. Some people say that he died of pneumonia or something. One of my uncles says that he was in a car accident, that he injured his liver, and later died of cancer. Many people who knew him say that he was very good to his brothers and sisters, very generous, and before he died he gave them a lot of money. I guess he was a good man. Anyway, tía Serafina had her son with her for more than a year before he died. And here she is in this picture, Leopoldo said.

—Can you imagine, Miguel! Only ten years old! That is why I tell you, hijo, *cuando nace una niña o un niño, uno nunca sabe cómo va a salir.* When a child is born no one knows what she will grow up to be like. *Sí señor, así es la vida. No mentira.* By the way, I won a lot of money playing poker that night. If I close my eyes I can still see that picture taken when Leopoldo's aunt was only ten years old.

III

A FUNERAL IN GUADALAJARA, MEXICO

Sighing, Miguel's father placed his arm inside of his son's arm. That day the old man was full of stories and philosophical reflections. Arm in arm, like two mature university professors, father and son continued their walk through the Mexican cemetery. With a gentle pressure on his son's arm the older man guided the younger man in the direction toward which he now raised the other arm. *Y allá, hijo ... .*

—And over there, son, in that grave is buried another man who told me a very interesting story, Antonio said, about an uncle from Guadalajara. His own story is important too, in his case, because of the way that he died after being a hero in the war. But the story about his uncle shows how strange life can be. Come, let's walk over there. Can you read his name from here? I cannot, but his name was ... .

—Sí, Papá. Efraín Silva.

—*¡Ajá!* That was his name. A World War II hero. After the war he got used to being called Silva, like in the army, he said. He was named after an uncle who lived in Guadalajara, the one that he told me about. Silva received a big decoration in the army, what do they call it? *Una medalla ... ¡de algo, no sé.* A medal ... I don't know!

—Are you referring to the Congressional Medal of Honor?

—That's it, sí, he was a big hero in the war. What a tragedy! Just a few years after he was discharged from the army he went to a dance, and he was killed. A jealous man got drunk because the woman he wanted to marry loved someone else. He killed Efraín without even knowing him. Young Efraín, who didn't get killed in the war, was in the wrong place at the wrong time. The man who killed him just got drunk because he was heartbroken. I was not at the dance, but I heard about the shooting from don Pancho. You remember him from when we lived in the house near the *arroyo*, *¿verdá?* Don Pancho was there with his wife and his daughter Elsa. He saw everything. The woman that the man loved was dancing with her new sweetheart. What was the jealous man's name? Ignacio Solíz, yes. That was his name, the man who shot and killed Efraín. Ignacio was the son of Demetrio Solíz, who married Gertrudis, the youngest daughter of Guadalupe Corral, a distant relative of your mother. *Pues*, Ignacio shot the woman, and when her new sweetheart tried to take the pistol away from Ignacio, he shot him too. Then, when Silva tried to reason with him, the man shot him as well. The police found Ignacio later that night. He had passed out. They say that he cried a lot when he sobered up.

I remember young Silva's funeral, it was a big one, and many soldiers came and they put a big American flag on his coffin, and the soldiers fired rifles into the air because he was a big hero in the war. And they played the trumpet, like when Alejandro was buried. But this was years before your brother died. Anyway, at Silva's funeral I kept thinking about the gringo barber in Pflugerville who would not even cut Efraín's hair after the war, even though he was a big hero! Ah! but that is another story. I will come back to that. I was thinking at Silva's funeral how sad to die young. Look at the dates, Miguel. How old was he?

—Nearly twenty-seven, Papá.

—*¡Qué pena es morir joven!* What a shame to die at such a young age, he repeated, especially after being a hero in the war. I still remember when Texas barbers would not cut our hair, just because we are Mexicans. No, hijo, it was not easy for Mexicans in the old days, even for war heroes.

In a few moments the two men were standing on one side of Efraín Silva's grave. Miguel sensed his father's momentary silence. He anticipated a philosophically wise commentary, and he was not disappointed.

We learn a lot about people when they die. Secrets come out when a person dies, Miguel's father said. That is what happened when young Silva's tío Efraín died. The man buried here went to his uncle's funeral. Many people from Guadalajara came to the funeral. They knew the whole family, of course.

At the funeral they were all surprised, Silva said, to learn that he had two wives and two large families. His uncle Efraín, it turned out, had loved two women and he loved his children by both women. Ah, the heart gets one into trouble! The heart can love many times. There are men who can love many women, and women who can love many men too, good women. Mexicans used to think that Mexican women who could love many men were bad women.

People's attitudes change, but not for everybody. We also see on telenovelas that even people who are married sometimes love other married people. There are so many divorces nowadays. What is one to do with the human heart? We tell ourselves not to listen to our hearts. One knows better and knows it is not right. But the heart, ah! Some people are born with hearts full of love, and people think it is wrong. It is a complicated matter, hijo, as I am sure that you know. *De cualquier manera, hijo, pos una de las mujeres,* Magdalena, the one he married first in Guadalajara, was *güerita-güerita*. She was a white Mexican with green eyes, like many people from Jalisco. The other woman, Rosario, was dark, *era morenita*. She had beautiful full black hair and black eyes. His two aunts were equally beautiful, young Silva said.

Miguel listened without interrupting.

—Young Silva went to his uncle's funeral a little before the war. Well, he learned that his tío Efraín was a man whose business required him to travel a lot. Sometimes the uncle would be gone from Guadalajara on business for two or three weeks at a time, and sometimes longer, for months. His business took him to Aguascalientes very often. Then he would come home to Guadalajara and he would attend to his business there for several weeks, or months, and he would be on the road again. That is the way it was, year in and year out. Well, when he died Rosario and her family came from Aguascalientes to the funeral.

Don Antonio paused, shook his head, blinked his eyes, and taking on the role of the woman with a change in the inflection of his voice, he continued.

—I am Rosario, Efraín Silva's wife. These, she told the people at the funeral, are Efraín's sons and daughters. I have been married to Efraín for nearly nineteen years. We have a business in Aguascalientes.

Rosario had seven in all, three handsome sons and four beautiful daughters. Magdalena also had seven fine looking children, four sons and three daughters, each of them just a little older than each of Rosario's other seven. Young Silva was amazed at how much all fourteen of his uncle's sons and daughters looked like the father, some more than others. Some were fair and others were dark like the two mothers, but they all looked like the father, who was also fair.

The uncle Efraín, people learned at the funeral, already married to Magdalena, had met Rosario on one of his business trips to Aguascalientes, and seven months after they met they got married. Efraín then formed a second family with Rosario in Aguascalientes, where he opened another business office. No one knew anything until his death, at the funeral. Because he had to travel on business often, Efraín was able to keep the two families a secret from each other.

Only the manager of his business in Guadalajara knew. Silva's Uncle

Efraín would tell Rosario that he had to go to Guadalajara on business, for long periods of time. When he was in Guadalajara, he would tell Magdalena the same thing about going to Aguascalientes. When he died, his business manager, a trusted friend, followed the instructions that Efraín had given him to notify Rosario upon his death.

Both women had understood and accepted his long absences, that he had to go away on business regularly, for long periods of time. For nearly twenty years Efraín Silva led a double life. Can you imagine? He had two families. But you know, Miguel, what was really remarkable to the nephew was that at the funeral the two families met and the fourteen sons and daughters looked like brothers and sisters. But the strangest part for young Silva was seeing two of his uncle's sons, one from each family, only about a year apart, *uno morenito y el otro güerito*, coming face to face next to their father's open coffin. For Efraín the nephew, as you can imagine, *era cosa de maravilla*. It was marvelous to see them, he told me. You would have thought they were twins, Silva said. He saw them standing next to the open coffin, he told me, and every person at the funeral was struck by their resemblance to each other. Those who had known Efraín as a young man could see that each of the two young men was a younger version of the dead man. The two sons of Efraín Silva, *uno güero y el otro moreno*, stared at each other in wide-eyed astonishment, as if they were looking in a mirror. Then they embraced like brothers, and together they cried.

That is what the young man buried here told me. Ah, Miguel! Life is remarkable! *¿Verdá, hijo?* How many secrets do people take to the grave with them?

—And what happened to Rosario and the second family, Papá, the one from Aguascalientes?

—*Pues*, well Silva's uncle died without leaving a will. The only man who knew that he had two families, like I said, was his close friend and the manager of his business, the man who notified Rosario. Let me try to remember. What was his name? His name was Ru ... Rubal .... Ruben Rubalcaba. That's it. Long before he died Efraín Silva had told him about the secret marriage with Rosario. He had sworn him to secrecy, and he gave Rubalcaba instructions to notify and to provide for the family from Aguascalientes whenever he died. He gave him a power of attorney to do so, and Rubalcaba started preparing the necessary papers. But again life works in strange ways. Before Rubalcaba could carry out the instructions he had a heart attack and he died only eight days after Efraín Silva. *Pobrecita* Rosario. Probably her sons had to go to work, the ones who were older. But Silva also told me that Magdalena tried to help out the woman and her family from Aguascalientes, but Rosario became greedy or something. After a serious misunderstanding and a bitter court hearing, the relationship between the two women ended very unpleasantly. That is all I remember young Silva telling me. For years, I think of it now, I wondered what happened to the brothers and sisters. Perhaps no one will ever know if the sons and daughters of the two families ever saw each other again.

Miguel's father paused. This was a part of his father's storytelling that Miguel loved, when his father's mind seemed to be visibly pondering the meaning of life and experience. He loved to look at his father's face, deep in thought, moving towards a wise conclusion. Then his father continued.

—That is another strange thing about life, hijo, the way that large families go in many separate ways. Brothers and sisters have children, they grow old, their children grow up and have children, all of the same blood, and yet one or two generations down the line they do not know one another when they pass on the street. Have you not been struck sometimes, in all your travels, hijo, by a face that resembles someone in our family?

—*Sí, Papá. Usted tiene razón.*

His father was right. For the son, his father's observation had been confirmed countless times in many parts of the country, in airplanes and on buses, on the streets of many cities, at airport terminals, and especially one day, during the time of his tenure evaluation, when he rode the BART train from the Oakland Airport connection between the Coliseum and the Berkeley stations.

He admired his father's storytelling, his wisdom and his understanding of life in its myriad forms. Now, he was thinking, that was the way his father always told stories. For his father, human life always imparted lessons. From people's lives or their deaths he always found some instructive value, he always learned something. At the beginning or at the end of every story, and very often at both, it was customary for Miguel's father to emphasize a philosophical message or conclusion about human life. Miguel cherished his father's wisdom.

—And what about the barber, Papá?

—Oh, and about that barber who wouldn't cut young Silva's hair.

—Well, young Efraín had received a letter from the President of the United States—Truman, *el mero mero*—and one day after the barber refused to cut his hair young Silva went home and got the letter and took it to the barber and showed it to him. Efraín said he was going to write President Truman if the barber didn't cut his hair. The barber cut his hair all right, and after that young Silva carried his letter from the President with him everywhere, and when they wouldn't serve him at a restaurant or cut his hair at a barber shop, he used to pull out the letter and show it. That letter got pretty tattered after a while, but it worked every time. One day we went to the ice cream parlor here in Pflugerville where Mexicans could buy ice cream, but we weren't allowed to eat it inside. He pulled out that tattered letter and they didn't bother us when we sat down at the high stools. We were the first two Mexicans to eat ice cream inside that drugstore, right after the war. Not long before Ignacio Solíz shot and killed him. *Sí, señor*, he was a good man. Sad that he died so young. May he rest in peace. *En paz descanse ....*

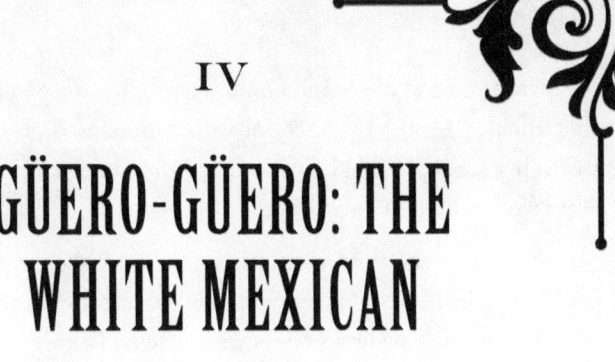

IV

GÜERO-GÜERO: THE WHITE MEXICAN

On the evening of the same day when he and his father went to pay their respects to his brother Alejandro at the Mexican cemetery in Pflugerville, Miguel was sitting in the living room of his mother and father's home in South Austin. His father's stories at the cemetery had moved him immensely. He thought how important it was that with his mother and father he always spoke in the language of his childhood. Miguel often thought of how his father had begun teaching him to read and write Spanish when he was just beginning to learn English. He loved learning the two languages side by side throughout his life. Using the Mexican newspaper *La Prensa de San Antonio*, Miguel's father had begun his teachings when Miguel was eight years old.

At that time he had been speaking, reading and writing English for less than two years. He could not remember when he learned English. It was as if one morning, in the first year of elementary school, he awakened and he could speak and understand two languages. In some classes his teachers asked him to help other students after he completed his own assignments with promptness and an intellectual understanding that astonished his teachers. From first grade, he was advanced to the second grade. He remained in the first semester of the second grade for only about two weeks, because he learned quickly, and he was advanced into the second semester of second grade. He remembered leaving behind a childhood friend.

Toward the end of second grade school officials notified his parents that Bickler Elementary School would be closed, and that children from that school would be transferred to Palm Elementary, ten blocks away from where Miguel lived.

At the new school, in third grade, his mind began to develop rapidly. In English classes he learned how to diagram sentences. He loved the class on spelling and penmanship. He had exceptional teachers in those favored subjects, and in art, social studies and math. A teacher with outstanding knowledge of each subject in those days used to teach the same subject to five classes of different students. As a grown man he felt immense gratitude towards his magnificent "old-fashioned teachers"—in the superlative sense of the word *old-fashioned*.

As a child he was fascinated by language, by words. In the third grade he became keenly, keenly conscious of learning that each thing had a name. When he spelled words on paper, printing them first, and later writing them in cursive, they touched his heart and engraved themselves into his memory. He wrote with a freshly sharpened pencil on which he loved a good, smooth fine point. The mingled smells of wood shavings, lead, and machine oil whenever he sharpened his pencil intoxicated him. Many years later he discovered other materials with their own distinctive smells, which he would remember to the end of his life. At the university, in his art classes, other smells—of turpentine and linseed oil, of oil paints and varnish—would be added to those he came to know as a child. In his young manhood he became fascinated by how smells, sounds, and images could conjure up the past, involuntarily.

From elementary school on, and because his teachers never made him feel ashamed of being Mexican or of speaking Spanish, he made a conscious effort to learn and to speak the two languages to the best of his ability, correctly, long, long before people began to criticize correct language, for reasons he would come to understand eventually. Correct language was perceived as being culturally oppressive. Fortunately for him his teachers were wonderful, old-fashioned English grammarians, middle-aged spinsters of German and Irish ancestry. They loved their students as if they were their children. Some of them spoke Spanish, and addressed him with endearments such as *mi novio*, and *señor*, even though he was a boy. His indebtedness to his father and to his teachers was immense. From elementary through high school his teachers nurtured his insatiable curiosity and his immense desire to learn.

That night they were watching a *telenovela* on the Mexican television channel. Miguel's father stood up unexpectedly and startled him and his mother. Something that he saw on television had brought back the memory of a story that his own father had told him. Miguel's father felt compelled to tell the story to his son, who was writing a book about the family. Her attention momentarily distracted from the Mexican soap opera, Miguel's mother saw the old man affectionately but firmly lead their son out of the living room and towards the kitchen. This was the place where countless delightful conversations took place each time the son visited, just as countless conversations had taken place in the kitchens of his grandparents' homes out in the country, in Pfllugerville, when he was a little boy.

His mother did not like for his father to talk when she was watching her favorite *telenovelas*. And she had let him know that in no uncertain terms. She would never answer the telephone either, if someone called during a *telenovela*.

In the kitchen, sitting with his son at the table, the old man began to tell a story in beautiful sixteenth century Spanish that a lifetime in the United States would never efface from his memory. In fact, the elderly Antonio Velásquez had amused himself by saying to his son on another occasion that Miguel's grandfather must have cast a spell on him, against speaking English, smoking, and drinking liquor, because in his entire lifetime Miguel's father never learned English except minimally. He failed utterly in using that language whenever he lost his temper; but unlike his father, he never acquired a habit for smoking and drinking. Even though the son knew that English could never adequately convey the beautiful Spanish that his father spoke, or the flavor of his storytelling, Miguel opened the notebook which was always on the kitchen table whenever he visited, and he began to take notes as soon as his father began to speak. *Miguel, hijo, esa escena que acabamos de ver en la televisión ... .*

Son, that scene on television about the Mexican Revolution that we just saw made me remember a story that my father told me. It was about an experience that happened to him before I was born, when my father was just twenty years old, about twelve or thirteen years before the Revolution. Whenever I see anything about the Revolution on television it always brings back memories about my father, and once I start remembering, other memories about my father come back.

—*¡Chingao!* I have so many memories of him! He used to take me everywhere with him when I was a boy ... . *Muchas veces ... .* Many times, I saved his life. As I told you ... *por mi tuvo vida mi padre.* If it weren't for me he wouldn't have lived as long as he did. I saved his life many times.

Now this story that I am going to tell you, I heard it from him when I was a boy. If I remember correctly, he was talking to me about how important it is to be always proud of being Mexican even if you live in the United States. My father used to take me with him when he would make the round of the cantinas. If he couldn't walk at the end of the night, I would have to carry him home, on my back. If he got in a fight I would have to make sure he did not get himself killed. One night when we arrived at the first cantina, he started talking about Mexicans who come to the United States and want to forget they are Mexican. We went into the cantina and sat down. He ordered an *aguardiente* and a beer chaser for himself and a soda for me.

The story that he told me happened in Texas, somewhere near Houston, around 1896. My father hated the United States and the gringos because of the war with Mexico, because they took Texas from Mexico. The only reason my father would come from Mexico then was just to make enough money so he could go back to Cerralvo, México and marry my mother, which he did. He never planned to come back to the United States, which proves that one can never know where destiny is going to take one. But like my sister, your tía Celia, says, our father's destiny was to wander. *Papá era de espíritu aventurero.* My father, and most Mexicans like me, dream of going back to Mexico. Somehow we end up staying here. Maybe one day if I can talk your mother into it, we will go back to Cerralvo where I was born, even if it is just to visit.

As I was saying, my father came to Texas and got a job with the railroad. He lived in a camp with other Mexican and Black workers. In the camp there was one Mexican ... *uno güero-güero.* His name was Juan García, or maybe it was Pedro, and the *güero* seemed to prefer the company of black men to that of Mexicans. Who can know why. He was *güero de a tiro,* my father said. He looked like a German, this Juan or Pedro García.

Speaking of names makes me remember what my father used to say, that almost every Mexican *varón* born in those days was named Juan or Pedro or José. Sometimes to prove his point, in the middle of a crowd of men he would tell me to be silent and to watch what was going to happen. Then he would simply say—¡*Oye, Juan!*—aloud, and among the crowd several men and boys would turn around. He would make us both laugh. *Te digo, hijo,* my father was a wise man.

Anyway, Juan García had blonde hair, my father said, white skin and blue eyes, probably like my mother's father, and also like Vicente's father before his hair turned white. Well, one Saturday, my father told me, this white Mexican Juan García went into town to get a haircut. All dressed up, *güero-güero* found the barber shop in Houston,

Texas, and he went in and took a seat to wait his turn. Juan noticed after waiting for nearly an hour that other men kept coming into the barber shop after him, and they were getting haircuts before him. Juan started to get angry because the barber was ignoring him. After a while Juan did get angry. He stood up, and he could speak English too. Juan talked to the barber.

—Look, I came in before many men and you givee them haircuts already. Why you no givee me hair cut before the mans who come after me?

—Sorry, the barber told him, we don't cut meskin hair.

—But ... but, *el güero* said, look at me. I have blond hair. My skin is white. Look! My eyes are blue, too. Why not? I'm white, like you.

—What's yore name?

And the güero told him.

—My name is Juan García.

—Thar ya go. You're meskin, ain't you? Sorry, we don't cut meskin hair.

Miguel's father was telling a story that the old man had heard as a boy, from his own father. At that moment, spellbound by his father's storytelling and by his changes of inflection whenever he spoke for a different person in his story, and amused by his father's occasional heavily accented English to simulate the barber's speech, Miguel listened without interrupting. Smiling, Miguel was imagining Juan García's English accent and the barber's Texas drawl. His father continued.

Well, hijo, Juan García got very angry because the gringo barber would not cut his hair. He went back to the camp, and he was furious. At the camp, he started walking around and talking to himself, out loud, full of anger.

—¡*Chingao*! Juan said, rolling up the sleeves of his shirt, turning his arms over and around. *Look! Look! My skin is white! Look! My hair is blond! The color of my eyes is blue! I cannot get a haircut because I am Mexican! Goddammit, I wish someone would tell me what is Mexican about me and I would rip it out of me and get rid of it!*

At this point Miguel's father paused, took a deep breath, shook his head in disbelief, and smiling to express filial veneration, he continued.

My father saw *el güero* baring his arms, holding his arms up, turning them around in the air, and he heard Juan García's angry words. Oh, *el güero* should never have said what he did! I have told you how much my father loved Mexico and hated the gringos. He could never tolerate any Mexican who spoke badly about being Mexican. *No, señor.* So my father picked up a shovel, and in a fit of rage he went and hit Juan García with the shovel, right on the back, knocked him down with that blow, and my father was about to hit him on the head with the shovel and he would have killed *el güero* if several men had not stopped him.

He probably would have ended up in prison, like I almost did when you were little and I almost killed a man with a brick because he would not give me work. We were so poor at the time that we had hardly anything to eat. But that is another story. I will tell you that one later.

In any case, even though my father was not a big man he was very strong, like your brother Andrés, so it took about four men to hold him and keep him away from Juan García. Standing over Juan García, being held by the four men, my father said to him, *jijo de la tiznada, your blood is Mexican, cabrón, and I will gladly help you to get rid of what is Mexican in you, your blood, pendejo, and I will drain it out for you, jijo de la … and if I ever hear you repeat what you said today I will kill you! ¿Entiendes?* My father was quite a man. And he was only twenty at the time.

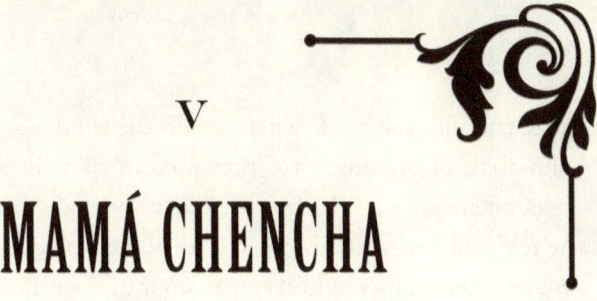

V

MAMÁ CHENCHA

Your baby brother Eddie was born in Austin, at the old Brackenridge Hospital. He's the only one not born in Pflugerville. He was named after my brother, well, he was really named after two of them 'cause I had two brothers with the same name. The first was Eduardo, *el güero*. Like many of my brothers and sisters he died during one of those terrible epidemics when he was about fourteen or fifteen, I can't remember no more, hijo. He was older than me, nine years I think. No, I don't have memories of him to speak of. I was real little when he died, I think. Then when my baby brother was born, my daddy named him Eduardo. Mi *hermanito*, the second Eduardo, *era morenito*, the one who married my sister-in-law from New Mexico. But come to think of it, I call him my baby brother, he called himself Ed after he came back from the war, but I had another brother, the one who died in 1925. I can't remember if he was younger or older. His name was Lorenzo.

But getting back to the house where you were born, you may remember it was a huge two-story house that looked out on the old Hutto Highway. Mr. Zimmerman owned it and acres and acres of land. My daddy was a tenant farmer. For years we lived in that big house, and we planted and picked cotton for Mr. Zimmerman, yes, hijo, acres and acres, as far as the eye could see. Well anyway, the big old house had an attic and nearly twenty rooms, more than we needed. I can't remember exactly how many rooms anymore, 'cause I'm old. Lots of the rooms were empty.

The attic and the second floor were always full of pigeons. They lived under the eaves of the house, and they used to come into the attic and into the house when we left the windows open for fresh air. Hundreds of pigeons, hijo! They used to come in to make nests, lay eggs, and hatch their little ones. When you and Alex were little—may he rest in peace—I used to take care of you, as you know, helping out your mama, and I would take you up into the attic and I showed you how to clap your hands to scare them away. Clap-clap and the pigeons would open their wings and fly up into the air, scattering and making a big racket, blowing dust everywhere with their wings. You can't imagine what a racket they used to make.

My grandma spent the last years of her life in that house when she was very old. Even if we were downstairs, we knew, hijo, from the racket that the pigeons made that she was out of bed, going in and out of rooms and wandering up and down the halls. The pigeons used to come into the house on the second floor. *¡Épale palomas!* She would scare them with her voice, and she would stamp her feet to make them scatter and fly away. Maybe you remember how we used to catch the pigeons, when you were little, and how Mamá would make soup with them, adding rice or *fideo* (vermicelli) and vegetables.

Lorenza was her name, your great-grandmother, hijo. We called her Mamá Chencha. She was a very dark, wrinkled old woman, real small, all bony arms and legs, and she didn't have any teeth. She had long, scraggly, white hair 'cause she refused to comb it, white as snow. You probably don't remember her at all, 'cause back then you were just a little bitsy boy. She used to sleep a lot, I remember, and bless her heart, she smelled of old age, best as I can explain it.

My grandma, bless her heart and may she rest in peace, she was like a child in her old age. She was over a hundred years old, hijo, when she died in 1938. That was not long after your brother Tony was born. I'm sure your mother remembered her too, when she was alive, 'cause Mamá Chencha used to go into little Tony's room and take his milk bottle and make him cry.

Mamá Chencha was born in Mexico. I don't know where, but I know it wasn't in Cerralvo where my mother was born. *Sí, hijo*, she lived to be one hundred and two years old, and a date sticks in my mind, August 28. But I'm too old to remember if that is the date when she was born or when she died. I was twenty-five in 1938, and that was a long time ago, more than fifty years. I was eleven years old when my grandfather Epitacio died in 1924, and I can hardly remember him.

We called him Papá Tacho. He was much older than my grandmother, and he married her when he was more than twice her age, when she was fifteen or sixteen. In Mexico in the old days, as my sister Celia says, a girl of twelve or thirteen was a woman. He's buried near Pflugerville, at Tres Puntos, close to Round Rock. My grandmother, Miguel, she's buried in the Pflugerville Mexican cemetery, like most mexicanos who were raised and lived in these parts. If you walk around the cemetery and look at the dates on the stones you will see that she was born long before everybody who's buried there, and she lived longer than all of them, too. I think that's a sign of good blood, hijo, that's what I say. Look at your daddy, my brother's now over ninety, and he sure looks good for his age. But if you look at the person's grave marker who's buried right next to Mamá Chencha, *pobrecita*, you'll see that she died at a very young age, two years before my grandmother. You can read her name and the dates when she was born and when she died. That's how I know where to find my grandmother's grave 'cause Mamá Chencha's grave marker is impossible to read. Some things I remember real good. Sra. María S. Rendón, born April 3, 1912, died on June 26, 1936. *¡Pobrecita!* The woman buried next to my grandmother was barely twenty-four years old when she died!

You want to know where Mamá Chencha's grave is? Well, if you're standing by your brother's or by your mama's grave, you just take about twenty steps west from there, and then about seven or eight feet to the left, *¡ajá!* That's where your great-grandmother Mamá

Chencha, my daddy's mother, is buried. After the Revolution my daddy went back to Mexico and brought her and my grandpa to live with us here in Texas. Next time you come to see me, if you like, I'll take you right to her grave. You can barely read the little aluminum grave marker on the stone, but you can make out her name.

The name used to be clear. Sra. Lorenza Velásquez, viuda del Sr. Epitacio Velásquez. Her maiden name was Ortíz. You can't read the dates anymore, but I remember them. Born 1836 Died 1938. I guess I'll never know if August 28 is the day when she died or the day when she was born. I'm old now, hijo, and 1938 was a long time ago. Did I already say that? My memory is not what it used to be.

¡Ay hijo! please excuse my sniffles. It's just that every time I look at you, I think of my father. He never went to school, and he didn't learn to read and write until after he married my mother. He had a good mind, like you do, and I'm glad you went to college. When I think of my daddy the tears come into my eyes. Can't help it. *¡Ay! hijo*, you look just like my daddy!

Miguel was puzzled by a recurrent dream of wandering through a great house. In the dream he was walking down a long endless hall-way, and looking through numerous open doors into empty rooms. The countless rooms seemed vaguely familiar. He could not tell if in the dream he is a child or an adult with a consciousness of a very vague childhood memory.

On that last visit his elderly aunt, Emily, helped him to make sense of the recurrent dream. Or did she perhaps create in his mind invented childhood memories of the big house in which he was born? What did it matter?

Months after visiting with his aunt Miguel dreamed of himself as a child standing in front of an open door, looking into a sewing room that was full of pigeons milling around on the floor. Some of the pigeons were standing on an old Singer sewing machine, and other pigeons were perched on the chair in front of it. Otherwise empty, the room was strangely illuminated by light that slanted into the room. Filtered by old, tattered, transparent curtains, the softened light cast corners into shadow, creating an unusual scene of light and dark and dreamlike mystery, and all of it was enhanced by the shadows of the pigeons standing in large, trapezoidal patches of light slanting across the wooden floor.

Miguel had listened to his aunt talking about the big house in which he was born. His dreaming mind now conjured up the striking image of his great-grandmother in his aunt's memories. The bent, wrinkled, toothless old woman appeared in his dream, smelling of old age. She was wearing a tattered long sleeping gown.

After the visit with his aunt, Miguel was amazed that one of his ancestors had been an old woman who carried a century of memories in some compartment of her mind. Those memories, surely, were buried deeply and locked away from conscious recall. They were inside her head that was covered on the outside with a wild mane of uncombed snow-white hair.

The mind's ability to dream is a wonderful gift, Miguel thought when he awakened from the dream. When his aunt was talking he had listened carefully. He had learned the exact year of his great grandmother's birth and death. The August 28 date mattered less, but it was more likely that Aunt Emily was remembering the month and the day when Mamá Chencha died in 1938. What really mattered to Miguel was that his aunt had given him additional pieces of the puzzle of his family's life. In her eighties now, his aunt Emilia *la güera* was the last of the elders on the fair-skinned mother's side of the family that originated in Cerralvo, Nuevo León, Mexico, dating back to the end of the sixteenth century. On the father's side of Aunt Emily's family the dark-skinned ancestors of Mamá Chencha were very likely from the Caribbean. Because of her advanced age every word that Aunt Emily spoke, every memory that she shared with Miguel, he knew he might not ever hear again.

His aunt had conjured up in the nephew's mind scenes of great visual power. Perhaps because he had seen too many movies or because he had read too many books, Miguel thought, his mind's eye had found the dream to be a logical way to embellish a fantasy memory cinematically. The dramatic contrasts of light and dark in the dream and the imagined close-up shots provided a playwright's ideal setting to bring a character on stage, and in this case, for the appearance of an old woman, Miguel's ancestor.

In the dream—he would not be sure when he recalled it the next day—the child, the boy or the man, stepped aside at the doorway to make way for his aged ancestor. Then the old woman began to wave her arms. She seemed to be in a trance. She added movement to the silent, visual spectacle that delighted his mind's eye. Then he heard an unanticipated loud clapping of hands—clap-clap, clap-clap!—and her voice. ¡Épale palomas! Instantly the flock of startled pigeons spread their wings and leaped into the air with a thunderous flapping of wings. Hundreds of frightened pigeons scattered and collided with each other in flight, slamming against walls, flying into curtains that now trapped and imprisoned the birds' wings.

When he awakened from the dream, he did not know if the dream had something to do with one of his own childhood memories, or if it was a dream that had given form to his aunt's story about Mamá Chencha, or his mother's:

A few years before she died, Miguel's mother remembered the old woman, Mamá Chencha. One day, his mother said, your grandmother Estefanita and I were in the kitchen, preparing the noon meal. Antonio was only a year old. His mother was making salsa, she said. In the molcajete she had just finished grinding the small, aromatic piquín peppers and the tomatoes, fresh from the garden. She had cut up the onions and was cutting up the fragrant leaves of cilantro for the salsa. Oh, the smells were unforgettable, his mother said, and he remembered. Yes, the smell of piquín peppers made him salivate. He remembered that in the old days cilantro was truly fragrant and delicious, not like the kind one buys nowadays. It used to grow wild year-to-year in the black, fertile, Texas soil.

His mother's very mention of the fragrance of cilantro thrilled him with a recollection of his young manhood. One day he and Natalie were walking, hand in hand, in the produce market section of Les Halles, in Paris, France. Suddenly he was surprised by the unexpected, aromatic, fragrant scent of fresh cilantro in the air. Pulling Natalie by the hand he hastened their pace, going past many vegetable and produce stands, letting his nose lead him to the source of the scent. The unmistakable scent of cilantro, strong and fragrant, made him ecstatic. In moments he re-lived many days of his happy childhood when his family used to visit their grandparents in Pflugerville.

At last he and Natalie arrived at the produce stand where he saw the cilantro. This is cilantro, he told Natalie, taking a leaf, squeezing it, holding it first to his nose and then to hers. My grandmothers always used it in their cooking. I remember liking it in scrambled eggs and in their soups. He asked the French woman: *Comment s'appelle cela en français?* And she answered. *S'appelle coriande arabe.*

Ah, *merci, merci bien*, he said, amazed to find Mexican cilantro in Paris, France, and chiles, too, hot fresh green peppers!

Since then he wondered where cilantro originated. Was it from here in the New World, from the Mediterranean, or from Asia? He remembered that one of the main reasons for the voyages of Columbus was that the Europeans wanted to find a route to the Indies, to obtain spices. One day he must look up cilantro in an encyclopedia He wanted to know where it first came from.

VI

JIMMY JOE AND HIS AUNTIE

W e were already in our sixties when we saw one another after about fifty years of not having seen each other. Jimmy Joe and I were childhood friends and we used to trade comic books. That is how I learned to draw, thanks to Jimmy Joe, from comic books that we traded, like Captain Marvel, Superman, and a woman of the jungle whose name I cannot recall. She was very important, however, because from comic books about her I learned to draw the female human figure, and from the other books I learned to draw the male figure. I learned especially the shoulder muscles and the pectorals and the stomach muscles.

Jimmie Joe talked to me about envying my "good hair" when we were little. Unfortunately, he was not a classmate. He told me of his difficulties because he was black. What memories!

He commented that his father used to beat and mistreat his mother when he was small, and he used to dream of growing up and killing him.

But I could not help remembering one memory about Jimmy Joe. I remembered vividly how one day he practically screamed with excitement, "Come on. My auntie is going to get dressed for work!"

Little did I know what to expect at first. His aunt, whom he called Auntie, was a stunning-looking woman who knew it. She was thirty to thirty-two years old, tall for a woman, and I would call her statuesque. She liked to dress up in fine, black silk underclothing that would set off her unblemished brown complexion. She was quite light for a black woman. Here is what he meant when he said that she was getting dressed for work.

When we arrived—two ten-year-old boys, one Mexican and one black—she was wearing a gauzy black slip and had just put on a sexy brassiere that revealed more than it concealed. We looked at the cleavage between her small breasts when she straightened out the brassiere, and we watched in amazement as Jimmy Joe made small talk so that we could look on. Had she turned to look at us his aunt would have noticed the lascivious look in our eyes and that our nostrils were flared. But to her, we were just two innocent boys.

We watched almost spellbound. Slowly and carefully she began to put a stocking on her right foot, raising the stocking up slowly and methodically until it was about seven or eight inches below her black silk panties. At that point she slowly fixed her hose with the garter belt leaving the smooth, dark flesh of her thigh exposed.

In the old days, long before pantyhose, women wore stockings that were held up with garter belts. One day, many years after I told one of the secretaries at work about seeing my friend—and long before the days of sexual harassment—I mentioned to the same secretary that when a man's hand reached the flesh of a woman above the stocking, he knew that everything was going according to plan and he knew what to expect. She laughed of course, in acquiescence.

We were watching, Jimmy Joe and I, as his Auntie smoothed out the stocking, straightening out the seam at the back. Her other leg was bare under the short black, lacey slip that barely covered her body. Her flesh was bare from her cleavage to the silk, black panties.

When she stood up and brought her leg down, stood for a moment on both begs, we saw that between her thighs the upper part of her legs disappeared into the panties and that there was a little part that fluffed out a little between her legs. She repeated the same procedure with the other leg while we watched, enraptured. Then she stood in front of the mirror and looked over her shoulder at the seams at the back of her stockings. Had she cared to she would have seen our reflections in the mirror and our eyes clearly focused on her pubic mound. But she was making sure that the creases on her stockings were straight while Jimmy Joe chattered on and on about who knows what. Who can remember now, and what does it matter?

All that I remember now is the image of that beautiful, statuesque black woman in her early thirties, her unblemished brown complexion, her beautiful legs and the cleavage between her small breasts. I remember too, her raven black hair, cut just below the neck, curled slightly, but shining with some kind of glossy hair treatment.

He told me many stories about his Auntie and her well-dressed friends.

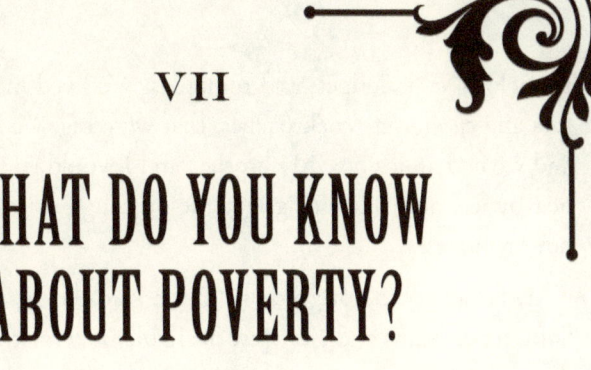

VII

WHAT DO YOU KNOW ABOUT POVERTY?

One day I was outdoors talking to our Mexican gardener. Something that he said or did reminded me of my father, who was also a gardener for nearly thirty years after he retired. I told him that my father could not find work because he was Mexican, and that he was saddened by his inability to buy groceries for his family of eight. My mother remembered that one day the man whose name was Buratti delivered a big box of groceries to our house by the creek. It included beans and rice, soap to wash clothing, and a broom. When my father protested because he did not have a job or money Buratti said not to worry. "I know you will pay me when you can." And my father did. My father was very grateful.

Buratti was one of two brothers who owned a big store on the East Side, where most Mexicans lived. Much later I learned that they loved the Mexican women who came into the store, and of course they were beautiful. The two brothers were also very decent and respectful. They always looked out for their Mexican customers.

In any case our gardener and I were talking about when I used to be poor. That was when he said, *¿Qué sabe usted de la pobreza?* What do you know about poverty or about being poor. All that I could think of at the time was that my father could not find work because he was Mexican. Later on, I remembered *el parián*, a large outdoor market where my brothers and I would go scavenging for over-ripe fruit and vegetables. We often brought home discarded over-ripe bananas, watermelons, cantaloupes, and tomatoes. We lived in a house that had rats and *cucarachas*, cockroaches, that were big. We had no electricity and we had an ice box. My brother and I would go and buy ice at the nearby icehouse and bring it home on tough string that we used to buy at Buratti's.

My father could not get work in the 1940s because he was Mexican. Sometimes beans and rice were available only for the children. There were no Christmases for the first six years of my life. I remember a little ice truck with plastic simulating ice. That was my first Christmas present, at the age of six. A few years later my mother had to give me a belt in secret so that my brother would not know. There was no money to buy him a belt too, or for other presents, and I was the eldest. In junior high school we would come home, take off our shoes and go barefooted, to save our shoes. We wore hand-me-downs, some of them from our better-off cousin Ricardo in San Antonio, Texas, who grew rapidly and outgrew his clothes.

Before WWII we started selling the Houston Chronicle, then during the war, we used to dig for nails, junk, beer cans, wires and we would sell them to the junk man, el señor Torres. A nickel or five cents was "500 dollars." He used to make us laugh. We started shining shoes for a nickel and later on, selling newspapers during WW II. Young American soldiers stationed at a nearby base were good tippers. Sometimes they would tip as much as a quarter. My father began to help us with large numbers of Sunday newspapers, the thick Sunday *American-Statesman*. During the week we would earn about $2.75 a day, each of us, and my mother would give us a quarter. My mother saved money that we earned, and eventually, around 1947 or 1948, we could make the down payment on a seven thousand dollar home where the streets were unpaved, near a slaughterhouse. We had an outhouse and no driveway. What do I know about poverty?

VIII

GONE THE CHILDHOOD NEIGHBORHOOD

Many times from year to year I visited the childhood neighborhood and the house by the creek, and walked the unpaved dirt streets. Each time that I visited Austin, Texas, something was gone forever: Bickler Elementary School was gone, but not from memory. Until the day I die, remembrance will always bring back the joyous cries and the laughter of children tossing books up into the air at recess and lunchtime, and at the end of the school day. I remember that when I was five years old I daydreamed of being among those happy children.

Today, gone are the houses of the neighborhood and gone from Red River Street: the used-furniture stores across the creek, the little Ferris Drugstore, run by an elderly Lebanese couple who used to entertain us with magic and make-believe stories, telling us our fortunes, what we children would become one day, and the future was so far away. Now the future is here and much of it is gone.

Finally, all the houses by the creek were gone, demolished and destroyed; gone our playground too, the unpaved gravel dirt road; the entire childhood neighborhood was condemned to make way for tall buildings. Over a period of time tractors came and razed the neighborhood; the land was overrun by dirt-moving heavy equipment; steel skeletons shot up; cement trucks came and went, they poured cement; hard concrete and asphalt covered up our childhood paths, banished the places where we used to play cowboys, hide and seek,

Red Rover come over, marbles or tops, football or baseball; gone were all the places where we used to run barefooted in the mud when it rained, and where we used to ride our bikes.

A great superhighway, the I-35, eventually brought great prosperity to the city, but destroyed our childhood world. Gone were the sloping hills where we used to slide on pieces of cardboard, at the park on East Avenue, sparkling in the old days with fireflies on summer nights; gone the favorite trysting places of adolescence, where long ago, we used to park our cars, first come, first served, among wild growth and trees. Oh, those places, always redolent in the mornings, with the heady sea scents of young lovers' nocturnal, festive sport, where as teenagers we heard the mingling of the river's running water sounds and the sounds of our first cries of love.

Instead of scenes of childhood splendors unfolding before the returning grown-up's eyes, great concrete pillars greet the eyes of travelers coming home, again; the pillars rise, hold up the heavily traveled superhighway; and farther south toward the Colorado River, how haughtily the concrete superhighway looks down now upon the trimmed green public parks at the Colorado River's edge, where only two or three years ago lush growing trees, wild weeds, and bushes waited for the tractors' leveling blades.

In 1976, when I visited the childhood neighborhood, gone were all the old houses except for one. How patiently did land developers wait for the elderly black woman to die, a homeowner without heirs, perhaps.

That year, and three years later, when I took my mother back, verdant trees and bushes and wild plants, a veritable jungle, had invaded the childhood neighborhood. Undulating hills that childhood eyes did not see covered and concealed spaces between neighbors' houses where we used to play.

And beyond the neighborhood I saw stretching out and round the entire city away from the Capitol, tall modern government buildings, skyscraper business office buildings, banks and great apartment complexes, and I wondered. Who knows what more will follow, what else will creep from year to year toward the childhood neighborhood? Rising upward, tall buildings were blocking already more and more the view of the twin sentinels of my childhood: the dome of the Capitol building and the tower of the University of Texas. One day, I thought, they will no longer greet the eyes that contemplate the Austin skyline, save from the air.

And on that day in 1976, walking through this strangely once familiar place where some of my childhood is buried now, I began to search for some recognizable signs of the old childhood neighborhood.

A year before that, I remembered, I could still take the same old path next to where our house by the creek used to be, down to the rocks and crevices of the creek, *el arroyo*—which we children never knew had a name—and walk among and through overgrown bushes, chinaberry trees, brush and weeds, all nourished by plentiful Texas rains.

Not knowing what I was looking for, unable to fit memory's mental image to the scene before my eyes, in vain I sought I know not what. While I was trying to place myself in the familiar surroundings of days that are no more, I turned around and unexpectedly, the top of a great pecan tree seized my attention like a haunting vision. The pecan tree was standing where I knew that the next-door neighbor's backyard used to be. Majestically the pecan tree rose high above overgrown bushes and chinaberry tree shoots, its trunk and lower branches barely visible among the lushly growing foliage.

I closed my eyes and directed all the concentration of my mind upon the pecan tree, and waited. In but a moment the tree worked its magic and brought back many scenes of my childhood. With closed eyes I saw again: there was the fence, a gate, and there the chinaberry trees at the edge of our neighbors' and our own backyard; over there our old dilapidated house and between it and the creek wall, the space where my father used to park the Model A.

I saw my mother, young again, scrubbing hard on the tin surface of a washboard. In moments the seasons passed in procession. I saw my mother, year in and year out washing clothes outdoors in all kinds of weather, hanging them out on the clothesline. I heard the sound of the axe and I saw my father, also young again, chopping wood for fire to heat the water, for my mother to wash the clothes, and for the wood burning stove. Whack! Whack! Whack!

I also saw my youngest infant brother taking his first steps, I saw clothes hanging and billowing on the line. I opened my eyes and at my feet I saw a huge, beautiful, wild *piquín* pepper plant, and the plant brought back the sweet aroma of my mother's cooking, the scent of chile piquín (we also called it *chile del monte*) or serrano peppers, freshly ground in the *mólcajete*, with fresh and sometimes fragrant canned tomatoes. Later she would mix the ground chiles with fresh chopped onions and wild growing cilantro, and I heard the sounds of beans sizzling in a pan, I inhaled the unforgettable smells of *fideo con carnitas* swimming in aromatic tomato, garlic and cumin sauce. All this and more the pecan tree and a wild piquín pepper plant conjured up, growing where we boys of the neighborhood used to play marbles.

Then, in my mind's eye, all the grownups of the neighborhood were young once more, and all the boys and girls were children, too. Across the distance of many years, in memory I heard our young mothers' voices calling our names when we were little boys and girls.

IX

SHE DREAMED OF SQUIRRELS

It was always a hazard, both professional and personal, for Miguel to read a novel or a collection of short stories or to watch a film about love. Did he really understand the characters and the events in the books and films? Or was he simply interpreting the novels and films in accordance with his own experience? And perhaps, was it more so in accordance with fantasies that had never come to be?

In childhood he developed a passion for books and later for movies. As a boy, he could remember going from one movie theater to the other and being puzzled to find at the other theater in the second movie that the man who had been killed in the first cowboy movie was alive again. He loved movies that ended with the crooks getting punished or killed, movies that ended with the hero kissing a beautiful woman or riding off into the sunset. It was very comforting to see movies that showed that people valued honesty and fairness, justice and truth, like he was learning at school.

It was inevitable that one day he would see for the first time a movie without a happy ending. He was still in high school. He went alone to see a movie that had a powerful effect on him, awakening in him powerful longings. Was that the depiction of a kind of tragedy that life would hold out for him eventually? Was that what life was like? Eyes smarting, his heart racing, he wanted to step into the screen and make love to the beautiful young woman who was dying in the arms of the man she loved and who had rejected her. The tears came freely when he walked out of the Paramount Theatre. He walked hastily, almost ran, to get away from the large crowd coming out of the movie theatre. The theme song of the movie would haunt him for years.

Ruby, you're like a dream .... You don't know right from wrong ....

Years later in his young manhood, he acquired the habit of becoming the character of whatever book he happened to be reading, or of the movie he was watching on the screen. It was not unusual to imagine himself as a writer or as Guido Anselmi, a filmmaker. He could, for example, be an Italian director one day, making an autobiographical film about the making of a film, based on his childhood, his erotic fantasies, and his work as a filmmaker. On another day he could just as easily imagine himself as the character, the Japanese lover of a French actress who is visiting his home in Hiroshima. Or he could become the artist Johann in a Swedish film, descending into madness, nostalgically indulging in fantasies of necrophilia with a former mistress.

The camera captures Johann from a low angle. He stands facing the camera, looking down at his beautiful dead mistress. She lies on a bier, eyes closed. The delirium and anguish in his eyes is not unfamiliar. He lifts the sheet away from the beautiful naked body of his (presumably) dead mistress (whom he has not seen in five years).

His hand comes alive and runs gently, with infinite tenderness, across her naked body, over one small breast, downward across the rib cage, down over the shallow landscape of her belly. ... Momentarily the man's hand rests on her pubic hair, passes down, turns with fingers downward, and moves in between her legs. At that moment the woman opens her eyes, rises to a sitting position and bursts into a loud, mocking laughter whose effect becomes clearly evident on the now deranged face of the artist whose hand was mournfully reminding him of the pleasures of days gone by.

Other times Miguel becomes the unfaithful, the adulterous Italian husband of Luisa in one film or of Giuletta in another film. On many occasions in addition, he becomes Joseph K who journeys across the daily nightmare of a labyrinthine maze of bureaucracy. Joseph knows well the absurdity of life.

One of Miguel's favorite roles is that of Harry Haller; another, Walter Mitty. The role of Rango also attracts him. Rango, Caribbean drummer, whose hands caress and draw sensual pleasure from the skin of his drum instruments. He awakens desire in a woman in the audience, at the café where he plays. Fascinated with his African ancestry, she imagines his hands drawing music from the flesh of her belly.

He was each of them. Miguel was aware of the mysterious power of songs that enabled him to become other men. Again and again he read in one of his favorite books the passage where the man speaks:

Ton mari, il sait cette histoire?

No, she answers.

Il n'y a que moi, alors? he asks.

Yes, you are the only one who knows. My husband does not know about our love. Lovers have no need for secrets. I have no reason to lie to you, she says.

By then, in the film, her first lover and the present one have become one and the same man. The present lover, like the woman's first lover, will remain a secret to the husband. What does it matter whether she will stay in his city or go back to Paris? At the end of the film they are not a man and a woman, they are two cities, and their love story has become a song, only a poem, as if that were something insignificant.

At the age of twenty-nine, with a natural propensity to follow his feelings and thoughts of the moment far into the future and to trace their logical consequences with insightful accuracy, he was inspired by the love of an older woman. He foresees when he is not yet thirty, and begins to write a novel about an impossible love between an older man and a young woman half his age.

Years later, in his forties and still trying to write a novel, he dates a notebook entry, April 4. The year is omitted. At that time the character of his novel was apparently giving him difficulties.

My fictional character, he writes, will live out my wildest fantasies, my most delirious desires, my most exquisite passions. I am going to have him fall hopelessly, irremediably in love. And he will suffer for making me suffer with his impossible demands as a character!

He continued to read the book that had turned his thoughts to the young woman who was half his age. *Dans quelques années, quand je t'aurai oubliée, et que d'autres histoires comme celle-lá … par la force de l'habitude, arriveront encore, je me souviendrai de toi comme de l'oubli de l'amour même. Je penserai … cette histoire comme … l'horreur de l'oubli. Je le sait déjà ….*

He made another entry in his notebook.

A book, written by a woman, has fallen into my hands. Her writing leaves me breathless. Is it revenge on men that motivate her female protagonists? The writer? No. Her writing celebrates womanhood, the female body, the source of woman's power over men. A magical power. But the women in her stories are more than female bodies. Their bodies are houses of the spirit. A woman's body has infinite powers, magical, mystical powers. Body and spirit, a woman knows how to love, to comfort, and above all, to make men gentle and tender. This woman writer turns relationships between women and men into poetry.

Some of her female characters remind me of Nicollette, and of Héloise, beloved women of the dying pilgrim and of Abélard, respectively.

Undeniably our bodies are a miracle of nature. What a marvelous change to which men and women awaken each other on the one day when together we cross the bridge, irrevocably, and find ourselves in that other world of men and women, where we shall dwell thereafter. After years and months and weeks and hours of fear and trepidation we are there.

In the case of a woman, how amazing the miracle that takes place, one day, the first time, after having to go to the bathroom repeatedly, not knowing why, being eleven or twelve years old, feeling tired, restless, inexplicably uncomfortable .... And the great miracle of womanhood, puberty, arrives.

As a father I will always remember. I was there when my daughter was twelve years old .... Daddy ... Daddy, *the child said, trembling in my arms ...* it started *.... I took her and held her in my arms and we wept together. Oh my honey, you are a woman now, and I told her that she could now have babies and she rested in my arms, just as she did when she was a newborn child, and I will never forget what it felt like to hold the trembling child who just then had become a woman. Oh, my honey,* hijita preciosa. *Be proud always of being a woman.*

He remembered. The young woman half his age had told him about girls' adolescent curiosity. Girls wondering, asking each other if they would ever do any of the things with boys that are rumored that girls do .... One night, *she said,* I came home and found my brother and my sister-in-law ... in the living room, on the carpet ... they were making out ... she was making funny sounds ... I pretended not to notice.

Cariño, *I remember you like Rolf Carlé remembers Eva Luna, the way that Horacio Oliveira remembers la Maga, and the way that Baudelaire remembers* une passante:

Fugitive beauté, dont le regard m'a fait soudainement renaître,
Ne te verrai-je plus que dans l'éternité?

Ailleurs, bien loin d'ici! trop tard! jamais peut-être!
Car j'ignore où—tu fuis, tu ne sais où—je vais,
O toi que j'eusse aimée, toi qui le savais!

I can hear your voice, Helena, and I am full of recollections of you, of us. You taught me to laugh again. But for the memories and the letters I might now be beginning to forget. In order never to forget, I write our story. Miguel, *you said.*

Miguel, I was moved by pity or sympathy, but there was selfishness on my part too. At first I just wanted to use you, to know what sex was like. I asked myself. Why not do one another a favor? I never thought it could ever be anything more than just an experience. I was afraid of you at first, I told you. Never having had sex, how could I have known that sex could be more than sex with someone that you knew ... well, that the relationship could never ... well, you know, go anywhere. So I thought about it. You were older and you were married. In a year or two I would be leaving. It was ideal for me. No entanglements, no possessiveness, Why not? So I decided to let you cure me of my virginity. Yes, we can be amused by my saying this. I am glad you smiled when I said it. You impressed me so much with the way that you deflowered me, because I was terrified. I thought it would be very painful .... Remember, Miguel? You got on your back. You said, drop down slowly on me. If it hurts, stop .... I drove back to my apartment and I called my sister. I did it! I did it! I said. I had sex! Really!

We were already beginning to talk about our love as it if were behind us. We had a love story to tell, a story of an impossible love that had to end. We talked a lot in the weeks before you went away, Helena, right up to the last few days.

I remember the dream that you had, and told me, nine days before you went away. We met in the early afternoon for lunch at the usual place. I arrived first and waited. You arrived and you pretended to be your usual cheerful self. I can close my eyes and see you walking toward where I was sitting. You are wearing a long yellow dress that does not conceal your nearly naked body inside. You wear no bra, only your bikini panties. You are holding a glass of iced tea in your hand. You tilt your head, smile, and take a sip through the straw.

—Hi! Would you like to hear my latest dream?

Those were the words that you spoke when I stood to greet you. You know that I love to hear people's dreams. We did not always hug in public, but we hugged. I said yes, very much so, and you sat down. Do you remember?

You made me promise not to be hurt and I wondered what the dream meant to you. You stirred the large glass of tea with the straw, while you collected your thoughts. You lowered your face toward the tea and sipped. Then you took the slice of lemon that was floating at the top of the tea and brought it to your mouth, flirtatiously. You took a small bite of the lemon. Then, squinting, you began to tell me the dream.

I dreamed that I was walking through the outdoor patio between the apartment buildings where I live. When I arrived at the area behind the Neighborhood Cantina I came upon two men who were sleeping on the ground. One of them was naked and lying on his stomach. I liked the naked man's body. Next to him on the ground and separated from his body were his genitals. I guess they were his. I felt a strange sensation of horror when I saw them, but at the same time it was humorous to see the man's family jewels separated from his body. I laughed to myself. The two men were asleep so I picked up the genitals, took them to the apartment and showed them to Julia. We both laughed. Holding the penis in my hands it began to get larger, and when it became swollen and erect I thought of inserting it, wanting to feel it inside of me, but I didn't. I just couldn't bring myself to do it. I kept the penis and the testicles for a long time, until they got old. Then I threw them to the squirrels. I watched the squirrels scurrying after them, and after the squirrels got the penis I woke up.

We looked into each other's eyes. Perhaps you were searching, cariño, for a little sadness in the older man's eyes. Maybe you were looking for some indication of hurt. But I was smiling, so it was hard for you to tell. It was a wonderful, a marvelous dream, I told you. Then I asked you what you thought it meant.

Today, it occurs to me that you may not have known what to do or say had you found sadness on my face. Again I said that it was truly a *marvelous dream, and what do you think the dream means?*

—Wel-l-l ....

You paused a while, and knowing you, not wanting ever to hurt anyone, you were perhaps debating whether to be honest or not. I am glad that you chose to be honest.

—Probably it expresses penis envy. I'm impressed with men's endowments, and I wonder what it's like to carry all that around, the scrotum and the testicles and the penis that can get so large .... Maybe it means I'd like to be sexually endowed, like men .... I don't know. I do know that at times I would prefer to fill than to be filled ... so I guess sometimes I envy men. Maybe I'd like to make love without getting involved with a man ... kind of take him or leave him. At least the thought's there ... kinda cold-blooded though, but I'm being honest. I guess that's why I thought of inserting it, huh? But I couldn't do it ... so that means probably the involvement's important to me. I guess Julia appears in my dream because she's my roommate, and she knows about us. I think she'd like to know some of the details ... even though she doesn't ask ... I know I'd like to know if I were in her place, but she probably wouldn't tell me and I don't kiss and tell either. You know that. Maybe she's in the dream too because of our conversations, the playful ones about women that I told you about. I guess there's still a lot of curiosity about woman making love with women. I told you about our talks .... Then, in the dream, the penis gets old ... so I throw it away .... (You paused for a long time.) That's about us, huh? Throwing away our love, huh Miguel? I'm probably thinking about how I'm going away ... maybe how I'll find a younger man to take your place after I'm gone, but I don't understand the part about the squirrels.

Cariño, *I did not interrupt or respond to any of your questions and conjectures. You were, you are still, no doubt, an engaging storyteller. It was always a joy to hear you tell stories during the short time that we had each other.*

When I didn't speak you continued after collecting your thoughts, as you usually did. Perhaps the times we shared together always flew by because you are such a good storyteller. Many times I told you that you should keep a journal. Anyway, I remained silent, smiling, and you continued.

—Maybe the squirrels represent all the young women who will get you, Miguel, if we don't see each other again. Ooh!

You became playful again, sensing perhaps that thoughts of going away and of saying good-bye were making us sad. And your warm laughter made us both laugh again.

—What if maybe I'm jealous?

I remember us laughing and going up to your apartment to make love. We crowded so much into those last few days before you went away, that I thought I would not need tenderness or passion again for a very long time. The time passed quickly. In a few months, from April fourth through August (the August date escapes me, but it is on one of your letters), you had taught me how to laugh again, Helena, and soon you would be leaving. But from that day on the dream became a favorite of mine.

I'm going to write it down, I told you, and include it in my novel. I will write that the older man began to tease the young woman who was half his age about the dream. I will have the older man arching one eyebrow and laughing warmly, he will say, well, my dear, and ask the young woman whether she is getting ready to throw him to the squirrels. And in my novel they will laugh and embrace and kiss and make love, over and over until the day that she leaves.

In my novel the older man and the young woman half his age will write to each other for a year, perhaps two. After that the letters will stop, and eight years from the fourth of April, when she was cured of her virginity, the young woman and the older man will run into each other again. He will ask.

—Did you save all of the letters that you received from your countless admirers who wanted to be your lovers before you came into my life? Did you save my letters?

—No, I had to destroy them when I got married. What about you?

In the novel the older man will tell the young woman that he saved all her letters, and his own, because he made copies of them.

I cannot say—he tells her—whether in the novel she will ask the older man to destroy them. I will decide when I get to that part of the novel. Perhaps I will read the letters one by one, and burn them as I finish reading each one. Maybe I will leave the letters for posterity, to let someone find them, long after I am gone and long after you are old and gray .... How strange and wonderful, to have known passion with a young woman like you, half my age, at such a late time in my life. It is a story not to be forgotten.

X

THE WORLD OF DOLORES VELÁSQUEZ

I t saddens me not to know what the doctors and nurses talk about when Isabel is not here to tell me in Spanish ... *me da mucha pena ... me da vergüenza y me da coraje*. More so, it infuriates me that in all my eighty-two years I never learned to read and write, not even in Spanish. What are they saying? *Estas enfermeras y los doctors, ¿qué están diciendo?*

I don't understand these nurses and doctors, or even my own grandchildren. I remember when my sons, Antonio and Eduardo, used to drop their children off to keep me company, when they were very little, before they started school, and later, after they started going to school, when they were ill and could not go. The children are grown now, but when they were little, I remember that taking care of them used to make me sad, to be sitting in the same room with my own grandchildren, like persons from different countries who are not able to speak the same language. Mexicanos lose the language in this country. I suppose it is bound to happen. Sometimes I would say something to the child in Spanish, to Michelle, for example, and she would blink her eyes and shrug her shoulders, and the same with Eduardo's little boy, or Antonio's girls, though they speak Spanish, but Michelle and her brother would say, "I don't understand what you're saying, 'buela." Some of the others, too. Well, at least they knew how to say *grandmother* in Spanish.

The doctor told Isabel that I have to stay here. Isabel, Isabel, I want to leave this hospital. I want to go home, but the doctor told her that I am too ill. He says I need medical attention that I can get only in the hospital. Isabel always wanted us to move in with her, but we were stubborn. She offered many times to take her father and me. When I wanted to move, Antonio did not. "I have too much work, *mujer.*" At his age, nearly ninety years old, and still wanting to work!

And the times when he was agreeable about moving, I hesitated, thinking about my mother in her old age. Getting old makes trouble for others, better to stay where we are, I thought. So we never moved in with Isabel and Vicente. Antonio and I could never agree. Is it too late, now? Am I going to get well enough to go home? Isabel is such a good daughter, no one could ask for a better daughter. *Si, ella tiene razón, pero* ... but I still want to go home even though she is right ... *pa lo que me queda* ... with what life remains to me, why not let me die at home?

I must have dozed off. Isabel is here almost all the time, but when she has to go to the bathroom, or when she goes to the cafeteria for lunch or to the house to sleep, these nurses don't listen to me. To them I am just a dying old woman. They probably think there is nothing more they can do, and they don't speak Spanish either. People in this country should at least know Spanish. There are so many of us who cannot speak English, but for us it is too late to learn. Not for them, they are young, and they should try to learn.

El doctor MacKenzie told me I have to stay here. He is a good young doctor ... *es muy bueno* ... and he speaks Spanish. *Habla español* ... he doesn't need anyone to translate for him. I told him I don't like it in the hospital, and he says, *"Lo siento mucho, señora Velásquez, pero usted está muy enferma."* He and Isabel, I know they are right, but I still wish I could go home.

Here in the hospital it is hard to get a good sleep. Sometimes I get drowsy, and just when I manage to fall asleep a nurse comes and wakes me up to take my pulse or to tell me I have to take a pill. Or a nurse comes in and sticks a needle in my arm while I am sleeping soundly and wakes me up. I look up and there is the white uniform, always one of them here to bother me. Except when I need them. No matter how many times I ring for them, that's when they don't come. I hate it when they don't come to take me to the bathroom and I soil myself. Then they take their time about coming to change my clothes and change the sheets. Is this any way to treat an old woman? Isabel gets angry with them. I don't know what she says, but when Isabel is talking and waving her arms and gets angry, the nurses listen!

Sometimes I wake up during the night and I don't know where I am. Isabel said that she found me in the bathroom the other day, cleaning the bathtub, thinking I was home. I don't remember, but she said so. During the day my sons and their families visit. Usually they take turns and sometimes they come at the same time. With their wives and sons and daughters. At times, the room is filled with visitors. My daughters-in-law, my sons, and my grandchildren, my great-grandchildren, but Isabel is always here. Sometimes I don't know who it is that comes up to me and kisses me and says, *"¿Cómo está, 'buela?"* What am I supposed to answer? Depending on my mood, if I feel like making them laugh I will say, *"Bien."* Then I say, *"Bien fregada."* All worn out, ha, ha! Ahh-a-ah! What a wretched life!

They see that I am dying, but they love to make me laugh with their constant joking. Especially my youngest, Eduardo, *¡Que lindo, mi con-sentido!* I used to scold him when he didn't visit me for a long time, always too busy with his work. He's a very important businessman, always dressed up, suit, tie. "I could die here at home," I said to him, "and you wouldn't even know, Eduardo. One day you'll come to visit and you'll find me dead." And in his playful way, he made me laugh, as he always does. "Of course I would know, Mama, I would read about it in the newspaper." *¡Ah qué m'hijo!* So silly. Always acting up. Here in the hospital I was remembering the other day, how right after he was born, when the nurse brought him to me to breastfeed, she said, "This little one gave you big trouble, a very difficult time, Mrs. Velásquez." A Mexican nurse translated, *"Este muchacho va a ser muy travieso."* He's going to grow up to be full of mischief. He is my last born. We were very poor in those days. He was going to be the seventh, but I lost the one before him. All of them boys, except Isabel. "No more after this baby," I told Antonio. "We can barely feed the large family we already have."

They grew up so fast. Now I wonder where the years went. How did we get so old? Who would have known that Antonio and I would live so long? Who could have imagined we would have such a large family! Every day they come to visit. Except for Miguel, he is too far away. If only he would write.

"¡Isabel! Has Miguel written?"

"No, Mama, but he telephoned. He's coming to see you, and this time Natalie and Sara and Becky are coming with him. Next week." *Vienen la semana próxima, los cuatro. Los periódicos dicen que viene un norte y que va a hacer mucho frío.* She tells me that the weather reports say a bad norther is bringing some very cold weather when they come.

"This is one of the worst winters in Texas in a long, long time. And you know, Mama, *Sara habla español.* You'll be able to talk with her in Spanish."

Que bueno, hija.

Last night I was thinking about what it was like to be a girl in the old days. For a long time I could not get to sleep. I was aching all over. *Pobrecita* Isabel. She had fallen asleep in her chair. If sleeping in a bed is uncomfortable, it must be much more uncomfortable to sleep in a chair. I finally fell asleep. Just before I closed my eyes I was thinking about Miguel's daughters. When the little one was five or six years old, I don't remember exactly, they came to visit. Her sister is a little older, two years, I think. Maybe they were a little older than that, but they were little. One evening the little girls made me laugh so much. I was sitting in my armchair, Miguel and I were watching one of the telenovelas on the Mexican television station. I heard them laughing, and out of the corner of my eye I saw them in the hall. Then I turned my head and saw them.

They were laughing, holding hands, going into the bathroom to take a bath, all by themselves, and they didn't have any clothes on. Oh my heavens! *¡Diocito mio!* There they were, little Sara and little Rebecca, just like on the day they were born, and I could not help laughing aloud. Miguel asked me why I laughed. He was sitting on the sofa and could not see his little girls. He asked me again. *"¿Por qué se ríe, Mamá?"* And I told him. "Your little girls, *tus hijitas,* Miguel, they just went into the bathroom. I saw them in the hallway, without any clothes on, just like on the day when they were born, and they were not at all embarrassed about their bodies."

Miguel told me that he and Natalie were bringing up their daughters to respect their bodies, to know that there is nothing shameful about the body, and that day, I thought, oh, how different it used to be for girls, for women in the old days! My mother was always telling us girls to keep our knees together, to sit properly. She used to get so angry about the way we would sit. *¡No anden enseñando sus vergüenzas! No se sienten como los hombres.* "Don't sit like the men do. Keep your legs together!"

So I am glad for Isabel, for my daughters-in-law, and for my granddaughters that some things have changed for women. They went to school, they learned how to read and write, and their daughters are in school now. The next generation of women will have good jobs too. My granddaughters take pride in their jobs. Whenever one of them buys a new car she drives it over to show it to me. "Look 'buela, I bought a new car." *Sí, me da mucho gusto por ellas.* They have good jobs. They buy nice clothing and dress nicely all the time. Yes, they speak English and they drive their own cars and they have their own money to spend. When a woman can drive, she does not have to depend on a man to take her anywhere. Things were much different in the old days. Even so, I always found it very annoying when any of my daughters-in-law or my granddaughters would sit down at the table to eat before the men, or expect to be served, as if they were men. *¡Me daba mucho coraje!* I could not help it. I never could get used to it. How dare they act as if they were men!

"*¡Isabel!* Did you prepare something to eat for your brothers?"

"Mamá, *estamos en el hospital.* We're in the hospital. *Los muchachos* ate before coming to see you."

XI

A LITERARY CONFERENCE

The two-day conference in Los Angeles took me away from the distasteful circumstances at the university. After the conference ended, driving home I thought of it. People from Mexico and California had come together to discuss the future of our Chicano literary studies. Thoughtfulness and warmth characterized the panel discussions and the social activities. Participants told stories that made us laugh. We spoke openly and laughed about how we perceive ourselves, carry out our academic work, and about how we feel and think. From time to time I would lose the thread of a presentation on account of one woman that I found irresistibly attractive and desirable. She was sitting to my right and I could not take my eyes away from her while a colleague was speaking.

At one point an elementary school teacher, David Arreola, was making the audience laugh with a story of a woman who had made a habit of coming to his office regularly. She was the leader of six mothers who came together and formed a pressure group. He told us that she asked him, Mr. Arreola, why are you always so busy when I come to your office? His response was that she had not made an appointment, which puzzled the woman. You mean, she asked, an appointment like with a doctor or a dentist? He went into more details, and even though I was half listening, I joined in the laughter of the audience. We were all laughing, but I was also imagining what I might say to the attractive woman. The conference ended and nothing came to pass, however.

Now the conference was behind us. A passenger in my car, Gerardo del Monte, respected my silence with his own silence as we drove through heavy traffic. He saw me negotiating the careless, speeding drivers moving in and out of car lanes, cutting off other drivers while I maintained a good distance from the car in front. Gerardo and I had met at the conference when I went to compliment him after his amusing presentation. The conference was one of those friendly *encuentros* when Mexican scholars and writers from both sides of the border get together. At the conference, while I was longing to hold the attractive woman, he too had been daydreaming of a woman, he later told me. Driving along, I whispered her name in my thoughts.

The brake lights of the cars ahead began to come on, and I slowed down. Then the traffic began to move smoothly, slowly at first. A little later we were beyond the places where major freeway arteries intersect, the pace of the cars in front of mine quickened, and I was able to use the cruise control.

At the conference I too had made the audience laugh. I told them of the first time that I made a professional scholarly presentation. A dinner banquet was organized at one of the most elegant restaurants in San Diego, California, with three after-dinner speakers to honor a distinguished Mexican writer on the occasion of the centenary of his birth. I was the third speaker, I told the audience. I was smiling to myself as I visualized in memory the large audience of more than two hundred people.

In my talk I said that we had been drinking beer and wine since happy hour started at four in the afternoon. We had an enormous dinner, during which we continued to drink beer and wine. The first speaker was mercifully short, I said, twenty minutes. The second speaker, however, must have had a forty-page tribute to the writer that we were honoring, and he was determined to read it all.

The audience listened politely for more than half an hour. Forty minutes passed. Forty-five minutes, an hour and more passed, and the second speaker continued talking. They had been without a rest break since before dinner. While the speaker who preceded me spoke eloquently of his admiration for the famous Mexican writer, I went to the bathroom three times. Sitting at the table of honor, I observed my two hundred odd colleagues. Little did I know that nine years later the events of that evening would become a laughable story to be told.

Now on the freeway a person driving a small Datsun cut in front of me to change lanes and then cut in front of another car to get farther ahead. I stepped on the brake pedal and the cruise control became disengaged. Gerardo and I were still both silent.

Last night, I told my audience of that evening nine years ago, how I could see with my Superman x-ray eyes all the little bladder and rectum sphincter muscles bravely holding forth. I could see all the distinguished scholars and luminaries politely crossing and uncrossing their legs to control the unbearable urge to urinate and to flatulate. How could the speaker not see? And my audience roared with laughter. Finally, I said, the speaker finished his talk, and the audience gave him a resounding round of applause.

By the time that I was being introduced I felt a great sympathy and pity for the captive audience. Had I not, after all, gone to the bathroom three times already? It was my first professional presentation. I was prepared to read my own thirty-page tribute to the great writer. It took many years for me to learn that professional audiences prefer brevity, unless one is a captivating and entertaining speaker. The captive audience deserved a rest break. So I told them before my presentation that I wanted them to take a ten-minute break. You should have seen them getting out of their seats in that great restaurant! Two hundred and more distinguished men and women rushed to the bathrooms, formed lines, evacuated their bodies. And fifteen minutes later, I had an audience of seventeen persons. My inclination was still to be merciful, so I took ten minutes to give my audience a synopsis of the long paper that I might have read, had it not been for the speaker who preceded me.

The laughter last night did not end there. I told them that the following day at happy hour I was sitting at the bar next to a couple of colleagues that I had not met. One of them, a thin, good-looking, red-haired man who wore glasses with very thick lenses, made a comment about the banquet speakers. I listened. Not knowing that I was sitting in the barstool right next to him, he mentioned my name.

—What do you think about that poor, stupid son of a bitch last night? Can you imagine anyone being so stupid as to let his audience go? I heard the goddamn place emptied out when he gave us a ten-minute break.

At that point, I told our audience last night, I introduced myself as the poor stupid son of a bitch who lost his captive audience, and we laughed so hard. My rubicund colleague gasped. He was truly embarrassed, and so were his friends. We introduced ourselves and I shook hands with all of them. They were all so apologetic.

In the car Gerardo cleared his throat. We talked for a while about the conference and exchanged pleasantries. We talked about women in our lives, as men do, just as women talk to one another of the men they are dating and meeting. Then he told me a story. I listened without interrupting him.

I met a girl in a brothel—he started out. Yes, a prostitute, and without bragging on my part, she liked me. Another day we met and she and I went to a hotel. She got on top of me, and for the first time in her life—she said—she finished. She loved having sex with me. After many years of tricks with men, without sexual pleasure, she enjoyed sex for the first time. The pleasure of having an orgasm surprised her, and we became good friends too. She told me that she was raped when she was twelve, by six guys! She is so very nice, very sweet. Why did she go into prostitution? I wondered, so I asked her. But you know, Mexican women, especially when they are poor, all they have is their chastity, so they want to save it. Well, that was gone! Her family was large and they were poor. What difference does that make? Even after having sex with countless men, she never experienced orgasm. The men meant nothing to her and she never felt anything. Not until I came along, she told me. I'm not bragging. I love her and I respect her. I do not blame her for the life that she chose. Did she choose that life or did that life choose her? We started to see each other often.

When I met her she was sixteen. She was just beautiful. Then about two years ago she met a guy and she got married. Did he know about her past? Yes, he knew when he married her. I was happy for her because she is a fine person. I thought, great! Now she is off the streets.

Basically, I believe in being faithful to my wife. But now and then, however, well, I will go to a whorehouse. I don't believe in love affairs or playing games. She knew that I was married. Our sexual and emotional relationship was simply wonderful, based on friendship, mutual respect, openness, and no complications. When she got married, it was over. A year later she got divorced. I saw her two or three times, but I have not seen her in over a year. I never asked her why she got divorced. *El vato* probably got on her case about the other men, couldn't put up with it. I never asked her, but he knew. He must have brought up her past. I was sorry that the marriage did not work out.

Are Mexican men different nowadays? I wonder. No, not really, I think. We are still very bad towards women. We still want virgins. It is horrible that we are this way. I wish we could change. Living in Tijuana I see that at the border things are changing, slowly, but they are changing. I am a family man. I love to be with my family. I don't expect my wife to always have breakfast or a big dinner waiting for me. I can do without that. I prefer that she keep me company, talk with me, and that there be mutual respect. I don't want to say, Look! Here's my check. Have my dinner ready. I'm paying for everything. Buy what you want. Just have my meals ready. No, I am not like that. I think that we Mexican men need to change. What was her name? You ask the girl's name. Alicia. Her maiden name is Gutierrez, Alicia

Gutierrez. She is very beautiful, but I have not seen her in over a year.

Gerardo's story about Alicia really touched me, and I told him so. Sex with respect is a wonderful thing, I said. That is why I have never been able to make friends with men who think of sex as a conquest, who boast about getting women in bed. Undeniably, we are sexual beings, and some of us look back fondly on our experiences, with gratitude.

His story reminds me of my youngest brother, Dannie, I said to Gerardo. He remembers well the first stirrings of sexual desire. He told me that when he was twelve years old he was taking catechism lessons in preparation for the priesthood. One day after a catechism lesson at Cristo Rey Church, Dannie stepped out through the church door. Before walking down the concrete stairs he looked all around. It was springtime, and the sun was out. There was a light breeze. It felt good to be alive, he said. At that moment, Lydia Cabrera was passing by on the way to catch the bus. When I saw her, Dannie said, she was twelve years old, like me, and she was fully developed. I knew when I saw her that I could never be a priest.

XII

THE FORGOTTEN LIST

Who would have imagined that Dolores and I would live so long? Maybe I will live a hundred years. After all, my grandmother Mamá Chencha was over a hundred when she died. But it's sad to see Dolores being ill all the time, since she was a young woman. When I'm working I think of that morning a few years ago. We were sitting at the kitchen table, and I could not get out of my head the thought of how old we are. I said, Dolores, I think Death has forgotten us. The good Lord probably lost the list with our names on it, and until He finds it He cannot give it to Death to come for us. She smiled. She may have been thinking along the same lines. She hardly says anything though. She's never been given to conversation. What a couple we make. I love conversation. I love to talk as much as I love to dance, and to listen to others talk, but not Dolores. After we go to bed, she doesn't want me to talk. Please, Antonio, she says, how can I sleep if you keep on talking? For some strange reason when we go to bed that's when my head is full of memories.

¡Chingao! I don't know what makes me remember. Who can explain why I need to tell my memories and the story of my life? They just keep coming back, the same memories over and over, as if the memories themselves were afraid of being forgotten. I think of my whole life when I am working. To me, it's not really work when I am in people's gardens, tending to their flowers, mowing the lawn, pruning bushes, or replanting flowers. Doing this kind of work relaxes not just my body, but my mind too. I remember the past, and I think. I work for a lot of good *americanos*. They have made up for all the bad white people who hated Mexicans in the old days.

Then, not long after that morning I started to have strange dreams, as if by saying that Death had forgotten us the dreams started. I wonder what they mean? Dolores, I said, why do I keep dreaming of people who are dead? She didn't say anything. Only Miguel can get her to talk.

I was already in my eighties when the dreams started. I know that for a fact because for one thing the dreams started a short while after my brother-in-law Francisco, died. He was buried on my birthday, on February 28 when I turned eighty, six years ago. The only one from our family who went to the funeral was Andrés. He is a forgiving kind of man, and he never held a grudge against his uncle for not giving us back the piece of land that I let him use between our houses, so that he could plant two pecan trees. Whenever you want your land back, Francisco said, you know, Antonio, that all you have to do is say that you want it. I didn't object when he moved his fence over into our land either.

That was the cause of the argument between him and Dolores, when he wouldn't give it back. The city was going to pave the street in front of our houses and make a driveway entrance at the curb. I asked him to move his fence back into his own property so I could make a driveway for my truck. He refused to move the fence, telling me that the law says the land belongs to a person who occupies it for a certain number of years if the owner doesn't complain. He was my brother-in-law, for heaven's sake, my wife's brother, and he was married to my sister Emilia. I took his word that he would give me back that goddamn piece of land whenever I wanted it back. How was I to know that he would take advantage of our trust and being my brother-in-law? Dolores got really mad and told him off. She brought up how Francisco and Emilia brought my mother-in-law to live with them after my father-in-law Alejandro died and how they cashed her social security checks every month and never bought her any clothes. Dolores said she was always wearing the same old dress day in and day out. She threw it in his face, What kind of son are you, taking her social security checks and never buying her anything? You should be ashamed! Dolores said. And Francisco asked Dolores why she didn't take care of their mother. How could I, Dolores said, with all my sons and my daughter living at home? Which was true enough, our house was small.

There was more too, between Dolores and my mother-in-law that Dolores never talked about, but it was there. You could see it whenever Dolores went to hang out the clothes on the clothesline. Her mother was usually sitting outdoors in the backyard that faced our house, getting a little fresh air. My mother-in-law could barely see in her last days, but she could hear the sheets rustle when Dolores went to hang them out. My mother-in-law would ask, Who's there? Is that you, *hija*? Dolores, is that you? And sometimes Dolores would not answer her mother. Why? I do not know. That's what I mean about Dolores. You can see when she's angry or mad at someone, but she doesn't say why. Well, after that argument with Francisco he got so furious he went out, got drunk and came at me with a knife. He was too drunk to do anything. I managed to take it away from him. After that he went to sleep it off. We couldn't trust him anymore after that incident. That's why we moved away from East Austin to South Austin.

One day I was pruning roses for one of my regular customers, in their backyard, and I figured out when the dreams started. The dreams started right after Francisco was buried on my birthday. I will never forget my eightieth birthday either, because some of the people that I work for said to me on my eightieth birthday—they call me mister Velásquez, can you imagine?—Oh, meester Velásquez you no lookee lakee eighty-year-old man, you lookee lakee seesty years old! And damn it, it's true to this day. The false teeth not only make me look twenty years younger, they also make me feel younger than I am! They are generous people too. Two or three of them gave me checks on my birthday, eighty-dollar checks. A present, they said, one dol-

lar for every year you have lived. Yes, they are good people. It sur-
prises me though that rich white people would call a poor Mexican
like me mister, me, a man with only three years of schooling, a man
who works with his hands—to call me mister! I've been working more
than twenty years for some of them.

I knew their kids since they were little. The little boys would follow
me around and keep me company. They used to offer to help me with
the chores in the gardens. I saw them grow up, go off to college, come
back, get married, and have children. I have seen many changes in my
time. I see young people when I drive by the university. A lot of them
look Mexican, and it makes me glad that more Mexicans are going to
the university. I'm proud of my son Miguel who is a university professor. I'm glad that he doesn't have to work like I had to work all my
life. More and more I think that if it hadn't been for the Revolution,
no telling what I would have become.

The dreams make me wonder. I guess I repeat myself. Dolores told
me she knows my stories by heart. Still, like I said to her, there's one
dream of my father that keeps coming back.

I keep dreaming of friends from the old days who died. I dream
of them as they used to be in life when we were children or boys or
young men. In the old days, after we became grown men, I used to
run into them no matter where I went. Eventually people that I grew
up with started to die. Now that they're dead they have started to
visit me in my dreams. I dream sometimes that I'm walking down
on Sixth Street where I used to work during the war, and I run into
them, looking just like they did in the old days. We talk for hours and
hours, but when I wake up I don't remember what we talked about.
The conversations when they were alive, those I remember. We used
to ask each other how our children were doing, talk about how important it was to send them to school, so they wouldn't have to work
like us. We would ask if there was any news about old friends. How
did Fulano's marriage turn out? Is Mengano still beating his poor wife

when he gets drunk? The years passed and we would ask each other who died. It began to seem that we were going to funerals once or twice a month, several times a year. Some of our friends died young, and they were a lot younger than me.

People tell me I'm too old to be climbing tall trees. They're afraid I might fall and kill myself, but like I tell Dolores, if the good Lord wanted me He's had many, many opportunities to summon me. Still, I wonder, Why? *¿Por qué sueño tanto con los muertos?*

Can it be that Death is still looking for the list with our names on it? What would Dolores do if I died first? Or, what would I do without her? We would probably have to count on one of the *muchachos*, or on Isabel. She has experience taking care of old people. *Pobrecita* Dolores! What a pair we make after more than fifty years together. We have children and grandchildren and great-grandchildren. It's sad to think that we have outlived a son, a grandson, and one of the great-grandchildren. May they all rest in peace. To this day Dolores gets sad when she thinks of them. No matter how many years pass, it is still sad to think that we lost them. There are times when we are watching television and I notice her eyes. I can see that it makes her sad to look at the picture of Alejandro. Ah, yes, Dolores and I are surprised that we have outlived people of our generation and many younger people too. That's why I say that God must have lost the list with our names. Otherwise, why are we still living? Either He has misplaced the list, or He is honoring the pact that He made with me long ago, when our boys were little, to let me live a hundred years. And He wants Dolores to be with me too. I don't want to live if I get sick. I never want to become a burden to anyone. If I get sick then I want Him to take me, swiftly, without suffering. Right now, I am thankful for good health. Only fourteen more years and I will be a hundred. *!Chingao!* What a long life Dolores and I have had!

And still, the dreams:

All during the night the boy walked in the darkness, among the chaparral, across familiar-looking desolate plains, across vast stretches of rocky land. In the morning the mountains in the far distance looked small. Their jagged outlines gave the impression that they were moving farther and farther away no matter how long he walked. His walk seemed endless. Not knowing his destination the boy walked on as if some matter of urgency were compelling him to go on. Another night came. The boy felt no need to sleep. His path was lit only by scintillating stars.

After the second night, continuing on at the break of dawn, seeing only immense distances, the boy began to listen for some indication of a town or a village. Slowly, it began to get light. He listened for the barking of dogs or the crowing of roosters. If he heard one or the other it would lead him to a town or a village. But he heard nothing. A while passed, then the sound of a man's voice broke the early morning silence. In the middle of nowhere, at the moment when the sun rose above the jagged mountain skyline, the voice called his name.

—¡*Oye* Antonio, listen muchacho!

Looking in all directions the boy saw no one. He heard his name two times, but still he saw no one. A few moments later he heard a horse approaching at his back. He turned around. In the middle of nowhere a man on a horse had appeared. The horseman came closer. He was wearing a Texan hat and the uniform of a cavalry soldier. A sword was swinging at his side. The butt of a rifle was sticking out of a leather case that was attached to the saddle. When the horseman halted, the boy recognized his father, and the boy cried out.

—¡*Papá, papá!* It is you! Where are you going, *papá?*

—I have been looking for you, hijo.

The next morning, when I woke up I couldn't remember anything of the long conversation with my father. As usual, I mentioned it to Dolores. It makes her mad if I talk about my father, so I simply said that I dreamed of my father again. I told her that if my father had not been on horseback and in uniform I would have thought it was our son Miguel without his beard.

Two years before Miguel's mother died he spoke with her for a long time on the telephone. Then she passed the telephone to his father.

—*Hijo, ¿cómo estás? Bien, qué bueno.* I had another dream. Do you want to hear it?

—*Seguro que sí, Papá. Cuénteme.*

—In this dream I am old, like I am now. I must have been walking a long time, and I am at the edge of a deserted town in Mexico. Has my wish been granted at last, I ask myself, after a lifetime of longing? Is this Cerralvo, Nuevo León, the place where I was born? Just a small distance away, between two rows of buildings, a small plaza faced directly the street in front of where I was standing.

I walked to the plaza between buildings of solid construction, like you see in picture postcards. They must be hundreds of years old. Almost all the windows have iron grillwork. The town gives the impression of having been abandoned. Reaching the plaza I kept on walking. I took a narrow street that led me to the edge of town where the land is fertile. From a cornfield, neatly plowed and irrigated, corn stalks were already shooting upward out of the black dirt. The healthy plants are a foot or more high. A little beyond the cornfield I saw the torso of a man resting on the ground, or so it appears from where I am standing. Maybe it's my eyes. He's too far for me to see him clearly, but he looks as if he lost the bottom half of his body, in an accident perhaps. Maybe his legs were amputated. When the man saw me he raised his arm up and waved, motioning for me to come over.

—I'm pretty sure it was someone I knew, a longtime friend, but I couldn't place him. At first I thought he had lost his legs, but no, I could see as I got closer that he was standing in a very large hole in the ground. He stopped digging and we greeted each other.

—*¡Quihúbole hombre!* What are you digging here? I asked.

—*¡Quihúbole* Antonio! Well, as you can see, I am digging a big hole. I've been waiting for you to come and help me.

It surprised me, Miguel. The man knew my name, and he spoke to me as if we had known each other for a long time. Even so I could not be certain who he was, but I didn't ask.

—I'm digging a big hole. It has to be big enough for two coffins. *Tú le puedes seguir ahí con la otra pala.* Here, help me. Take this other shovel and start over in that corner.

He was digging a hole in the ground like my friend Demetrio and I used to dig holes a long time ago, when we worked in construction. The hole had to be big and deep, *grandote-grandote*, the man said. He told me to start digging.

—What? And are you going to leave?

—*No, no, hombre.* Between the two of us we'll have it done in no time. *Entre los dos, como siempre.* No, he said. We'll do it together, like we always did. *Tú sabes.*

—I'm too old now for that kind of hard work. I can't do it anymore. At my age my legs, my knees, and my ankles are bad. They hurt.

But the man in the hole kept insisting that I help him, and meanwhile I'm trying to place him. Is he my friend Demetrio who saw me get buried alive when fourteen feet of dirt fell on top of me? *¡Chingao!* You know that story, Miguel. That was nearly forty years ago. I told you that I was fifty-one years old, working on the construction of the inter-regional highway, yes, the I-35. I'll never forget how old I was because it happened on 51st Street. Anyway, Demetrio, who witnessed that incident in my life, was my age. He died a little after it happened. Of fright, I'm almost sure. *Sí, se murió de susto.* I warned him, *¡Hombre, debes ir a ver una curandera o te vas a morir de susto!* He did not take my advice to go find a *curandera*, so he died, just like I said that he would.

In the dream I keep looking at him. Is the man Demetrio or not? Is this the man who worked with me until he died? He was only fifty-one, like me at the time. He should have gone to a *curandera* to be cured of the fright. He saw the dirt falling right on top of me, until it covered me completely. It was miracle, Miguel, for me to get out of that alive. I already told you the whole story. You remember. Anyway, many thoughts passed through my mind thinking of the dream afterward. Then I asked him if he was digging holes for sewer lines like we used to, or what? I noticed for the first time that we were in a cemetery.

—Who is the big hole for? Did someone die?

—Not yet, not yet. But we must be ready, he said. Come help me, Antonio. I already told you we must dig a hole big enough for two coffins.

Miguel, the next day when I woke up I was not sure who the man was. I had recognized him but I still don't know if it was Demetrio. But I'm thinking that it had to be him. If only he had gone to a *curandera* he might have lived many more years. It could have been someone else. I knew so many people in the old days. And I have outlived them all. I warned Demetrio. I told him to find a *curandera*. But he didn't listen. So he died. *Sí, murió de susto. Bueno, hijo*, I have been talking for too long. This is going to be an expensive telephone call for you. What is that? Yes, yes, hijo. I will tell your mother again that you love her. Don't spoil her though. You are far away. She misses you. *Sí, hijo*, and give our love to Natalie and the girls. You always make your mother happy when you call. *Adios, hijo.*

Well into his eighties Antonio Velásquez found pleasure in thinking that day by day, week by week, month by month, and from year

to year he was getting closer and closer to the age of ninety. His pleasure consisted in knowing that the closer he got to ninety meant that
he was that much closer to one hundred.

Increasingly, since he turned eighty, the old man's mind and heart
had turned again to the desire to visit Cerralvo. His was the same
unshakable dream that never releases its hold of the hearts of many
Mexicans who come to the United States and stay, the dream of going back to the place where they were born. The old man wanted very
much to visit Cerralvo, his birthplace in the *norteño* state of Nuevo
León, Mexico. Cerralvo is about fifty miles northeast of Monterrey,
only about an hour's drive from the border, Miguel told his father
years ago. We can visit Isabel, from her house we can drive to Cerralvo and be there in no time. My brother Antonio and I will drive you
and Mamá there, any time you like. But his wife Dolores was afraid
and would not go with him, and he would not go without her. On top
of that he too was worried that the customs officials might not let
him come back into the United States if he crossed the border. And
the years passed and he did go back, a year after his wife's death.

Of late, in his old age imagination and in his dreams a small town
or a village—perhaps Cerralvo—appeared to him more and more frequently. It may be that because he had lived in many places during his
long lifetime, surrounded by great flat open plains, and naturally because he could not remember the village where he was born, an image
of a town appeared in his dreams. The town of his imagination and
dreams combined elements of many villages and small towns where
he had lived during his long life.

In his long lifetime the place of his birth had become a dream village, a phantasmal place. At times vague memories of the child mingled with fading memories of later childhood years. Unable to recall
the village where he was born, that he had seen only as a child, the old
man's imagination and his dreams reconstructed and invented parts
of it. Assisted by all his senses his mind invented limitless distances,

an immense sky, nostalgic silences, voices that no one but he heard, whispers and muted sounds, and the music of running water. He may once have seen the gnarled trunks of enormous sabinal trees. These are the majestic, ancient cypresses that provide scenes of unforgettable natural beauty in a great shady park, to which families still come with lunches and soft drinks. Indeed, there was much to glean from his more than eighty years of life and experience.

The heat of the sun had nourished his body. He loved the sun in all seasons, beating down on narrow streets, rustic stone houses, adobe buildings, and barren plains. He knew how to find shelter from icy arctic winds from the north when they came sweeping down, howling insanely through the plains and the narrow streets of small towns. Not far from small towns, he knew, were silver mines from colonial days, now abandoned and in ruins. The northern part of Mexico is so spacious, its open plains left one reeling with a sense of immensity and solitude, and made one think of black-robed women sighing.

More dreamlike images quickened the old man's senses: fog, vapors, smoke and shadowy places, an old parochial church from the seventeenth century. In his childhood, listening to the tolling of church bells, he had strolled down narrow cobbled streets, seen low, modest colonial buildings, and a plaza and a park at the center of the village where elderly men come to sit on benches and talk. Close by or at the center of the park itself there might be a larger than life statue of some patriotic hero, perhaps of Miguel Dolores Hidalgo or of El Conquistador Anónimo. When school lets out the voices and the laughter of children, and the sound of creaking, rusty door hinges on a swinging gate bring joy into the hearts of those who are no longer young.

No one ever forgets the crowing of roosters at daybreak and all the scenes from the past that leap into our consciousness upon hearing them again. No one ever forgets that nights were once truly, deeply, inky black. The old man remembers that low growing chaparral bushes used to frighten him in childhood because of the phantasmal shapes that they took on. On these northern Mexican plains winter nights are so cold that the morning dew freezes as it falls to earth. In this region people still speak the popular language of Mediterranean ancestors that populated this area long ago. People who populated the area where the old man was born came with something to hide from the Inquisition. In two hundred years their progeny became part of the mestizo and criollo population, and hundreds of years later they continued to observe traditions whose known origins were lost. Here in the north of Mexico one is made keenly conscious of other human connections from before the coming of Iberians, human connections with earth and stone, sky and sun, night and day, and immense distances.

In another dream the elderly Antonio arrives at a plaza in the middle of the town. Enveloped in mist, the plaza is peopled with shadowy figures, elderly men and women who wander aimlessly, like figures in a Paul Delvaux painting, in slow motion. They are milling around as if they are waiting for someone or for something to happen.

A thin, lanky stranger with snowy white hair and black bushy eyebrows sees Antonio and calls out. The stranger's voice seems to come from another world.

—*¡Épale, hombre! ¿Cómo andamos? ¡Quihúbole!*

Momentarily, the elderly Antonio is startled and delighted, because he is always looking for someone who is willing to talk, to listen and to tell stories. Ah, if only Dolores would tell me her memories and stories, and listen to mine. Something in me simply makes me want to tell stories. I cannot help myself. I was born to remember and to tell stories. If Dolores would listen I would stop working and stay home. But she scolds me, saying that she knows all my stories and memories by heart. She wants me to keep quiet. Time enough for being quiet in the grave, and that is not far away. *¡Qué cosas!*

Except for her illnesses and not a few sorrows life has been good to us. *¿Quién hubiera pensado que íbamos a llegar a esta edad?* Who would have imagined such a long life for us? There is much to remember and to be grateful for. But no, Dolores is a quiet one. She is not given to express affection openly to our sons and our daughter, much less to me. I remember the day that she told me, *There will be no more children, Antonio.* Since then we have not hugged. And before that I never even saw my wife without her clothes. It is sad that she has been sick, for years, since she was a young woman. Having lived this long I think that He may keep his promise to let me reach a hundred. Dolores is younger, so He will probably take me first. After I get to a hundred He can take me any time. Like I told Miguel, the years from here on are a gift. Isabel or one of the boys will look after Dolores. That's why I don't worry about dying before her.

The stranger spoke again, and Antonio Velásquez thought, well, he might be a good person to strike up a conversation with. Still lost in thought Antonio shook his head when the man spoke still another time.

—*¿No me oyes, hombre?* the stranger asks. Are you hard of hearing?

—*¡Quihúbole!* Antonio said finally.

—Come and join us, old man. Are you ready?

The two men are about the same age. Not knowing what the stranger means, Antonio smiles and asks:

—What do you mean? What is there to be ready for? Is there going to be a fiesta, a dance? I love to dance, even at my age, but I don't think I'm dressed for a fiesta. Look, I wear these coveralls all the time, and these work shirts from J.C. Penney's.

—No, there is no fiesta, hombre, we are all waiting. We're old. Are you ready to come with us? Aren't you ready to go?

The stranger who is not making sense steps away from the crowd of shadowy figures and comes toward Antonio.

—What do you mean?

—What's your name, hombre?

—Antonio Velásquez.

—*Bueno, déjame ver.* Let me see, now.

The white-haired stranger pulls out a tattered, yellowing, brittle piece of paper. He runs his finger across a list of names on the piece of paper. His finger stops.

—*¡Ajá!* Your name is here, he says, right after the name of Juanita Vásquez.

—What does the list of names mean? Antonio Velásquez asks.

—This list has your name on it. It contains the names of those who are being summoned now. You are supposed to have your own list. Where is it? It was sent to you.

—I have no list of names.

—Ah! That's the problem. You probably had one, but you misplaced it, or you put it away and forgot where you put it. At our age we become very forgetful. In any case, we must go, in a little while. See on the list, here is my name, Rubén de la Cueva. My ancestors settled this area. Next to my name is the date of my birth, November 23, 1903. By your name it says you were born on February 28, 1901. You almost got to ninety, *compañero.*

—Summoned? I haven't done anything wrong. Go where? What does that list mean?

—*¡Hombre!* Don't pretend that you don't know, Ruben de la Cueva says. But I wonder what happened to your list. Are you sure you didn't forget where you put it?

—I never had one, I tell you, and I'm not going anywhere. If you're talking about death, I may be old, but I'm still in good health. Why I'm still working, almost eighty-seven, and before long I'm going to be ninety, and God willing I will live a hundred years.

At that moment the mist lifted and interrupted their conversation. It was night, and except for a single cloud the sky over the plaza became luminously clear and full of stars. Then a full moon pierced through an opening in the cloud, bathing the whole scene in a splendid light that brings to a traveler's mind the extraordinary reverberating illumination of freshly fallen snow on a misty moonlit night in great cities of the country to the north. The old people in the plaza began to admire their shadows, as if they had never seen them before.

The moon was of the kind known to poets and songwriters, a moon that makes lovers forlorn when they are far away from the beloved. It was the kind of moon that quickens the hearts of people who are dying and that reminds them of earthly, sensual pleasures connected with moonlight and music. Then the cloud moved and covered the moon. The old people lost their shadows and they began to search for them. No one but Antonio Velásquez was paying attention to the cloud that covered the moon. He was waiting for the cloud to pass.

—No, it's not time for me to go yet, Antonio Velásquez protested. I am not even ninety years old. Long ago I prayed, and He promised me that I would live a hundred years, and He will keep his promise, I know.

The next morning when he awakened, sitting at the small table across from his wife, Antonio told Dolores he did not know what his dreams mean.

Customarily of a cheerful disposition, the old man was saddened by his wife's declining health during the last two years of her life. Even though she was seven years younger, she had aged before him. His cheerfulness and his work kept him strong and active, and they had much to do with his good health. Antonio Velásquez hardly ever got angry, except when people were dishonest or mean. Driving his truck from South Austin to Pemberton Heights he gave some thought to the possibility that his dreams might be prophetic. On the way to work he thought of his wife.

Pobrecita Dolores, too many years of aches and pains, too many for one person. Now she has arthritis, diabetes, and who knows what other infirmities she has. I can't help thinking that someone cast a spell on her when she was young. *Sustos*, too. All those frights that she had years ago. I always told her to find a *curandera*, to get rid of the spell and make her well. She saw a few, but they didn't help her, and neither did the doctors. Crooks, that's what they are, goddamn crooks! After all those years *pinche* doctors never cured her. Not a one helped her, and the present doctors are good and kind, but it's a little late to help her. I wouldn't be surprised if the bastards didn't make her feel worse just to keep her coming back, for the money. Dolores never found a good *curandera* or a good doctor. Recently she started waking up at night screaming, saying that some men are standing at the foot of our bed, sometimes it's three, sometimes two, she says. Her screams wake me up. I've never seen anything. As soon as I wake up she says that the demons, or whatever they are, vanish. But they were there, she says. I saw them.

Pobrecita. An evil spell, I say. Probably since the days when we lived in that broken-down house near the creek, on the Calle Sabinas. She was frightened too many times when we lived in that neighborhood.

I was thinking of that house and the neighborhood the other day. I drove by there several years ago and everything in that neighborhood was gone. At the time the tractors and the bulldozers were razing everything to the ground. A few years later tall office buildings and a large hotel with a swimming pool left nothing of the old neighborhood. The pool itself was right where the neighbors' houses and the house by the creek used to be. It was easy to see exactly where the houses once stood only because they left the pecan tree standing where it always did in the Ríos' backyard.

The big hotel went up where our houses used to be, and who will ever remember that there used to be an elementary school on top of the hill. Everything from the old days was gone. The changes started when the freeway was built. To think that I could have bought that old house, property and all, where the hotel now stands, for two thousand dollars! Eventually we would have gotten cheated out of it. Maybe they would have offered us four or five thousand dollars. How could we know the land was worth millions of dollars? We could not buy it, of course, because I was earning barely enough to put food on the table for the children. Six children, only one of them a daughter. We almost had seven, but Dolores lost one just before Eduardo. I was working the night when she lost the baby. Thank God that the neighbors heard her screams. They came to the house, looked after her, and called the doctor. The fetus was very, very tiny. The next day I put it into a small glass jar and buried in the ground near the wall next to the creek. It would have been a boy. It had a tiny penis.

Dolores changed after Eduardo was born. *No more children after this one,* she told me. *Eduardo is the last one.* Before him she never said *m'hijito* this and *m'hijito* that. *Tan cariñosa con él.* All those endearments. I will never know how or why she changed. Maybe he looks like my father-in-law now, but she could not have known that he would look like her father? And I don't know that she had any special affection for her father or her mother. No one knows, as I have told Miguel, how a child will grow up. But Eduardo became her favorite, *el consentido.* Dolores likes to see him all dressed up in his business suit and tie. After he opened up his own office she was so proud he took her to see it.

Well, for not knowing how a child will grow up, Dolores and I have not done badly raising our children. The one thing we cannot change or control in them is the obstinate blood, what we inherit. In a large family one can reasonably expect that some child will turn out with a strong character, a powerful personality. Sometimes being born first, or just the name that we give a child makes a difference. Well, despite my father's blood and the Corral family blood our sons have turned out well, and Isabel, too. I don't know what we would have done without Isabel's help when the boys were in the military. The boys helped too when they were little. *Estabamos bien amolados*, as Dolores says. I keep telling Dolores, no one knows what a child will be like when he grows up. Working in my customers' yards, mowing the lawn, pruning roses, turning the soil, I think of Dolores. Now that we have a little money in the bank and can afford anything that we want her health is declining. *Pobrecita* Dolores, if only she were better. Who would have imagined that we would live these many years.

XIII

MY MOTHER NEVER LEARNED TO READ AND WRITE

Because my grandmother discouraged my mother from going to school, my mother never learned to read and write. When she died, that was my mother's biggest regret. I tell my literature students never to take their ability to read and write for granted.

¡Escóndete, Dolores! Anda, escóndete, porque vienen los oficiales de la escuela! Hide, hide, Dolores! The people from the school are coming. They want all children to go to school.

In the hospital, as she lay dying, Dolores Velásquez remembered her mother saying that a woman does not need an education. *¿Pa qué quieres estudiar? Las mujeres no necesitan estudios. Vas a tener niños cuando te cases.* Why do you want to go to school? You will be having babies after you get married, as many as God will give you. There will be plenty to keep you busy, nursing them, washing their diapers and other clothing, cooking, ironing, mending their clothes, taking care of your husband, giving in to his needs, and there will be much more ....

My mother always told us to hide under the house when people from the school came to our house. Only my youngest brother Rodrigo, who was a soldier during the war, went to school. He was the only one out of a family of eleven children who went to school. But as a child, Rodrigo, more than twelve years younger, cried because my mother would not let him go to school. He would cry and beg my mother to let him go to school. My little brother cried and begged, he cried and begged. To discourage him she would say, "The bigger boys carry knives. They will hurt you," she said. She despised his little friend, one of the Mercados, a boy who encouraged Rodrigo to go to school. Finally, my little brother begged and cried so much that my mother gave in and gave her permission.

She always told them that they were needed on the farm, to pick cotton, to pick the vegetables, to grow them, to help the men with whatever chores needed to be done. My brother went to school until seventh grade. In the old days Mexican boys usually went to seventh grade. Then they went to work, and if they saved their money, they bought a car and went after girls or got married.

Years ago, she remembered, her eldest son Miguel had come to visit and he had asked her why she never learned to read and write. He came that year with some kind of machine that could record a person's voice. He said it was called a tape-recorder. The tape-recorder had a little needle that moved when a person spoke. Dolores told Miguel about her mother's unwillingness to let her and her sisters and her brothers go to school.

She felt fortunate to have had too many children to look after her father-in-law or her mother-in-law in old age, as was the Mexican custom in the old days. Consequently, my father's sister, who only had one son, took care of my paternal grandparents in their old age. My mother's brother, my *tío* José, and my *tía* Emily took in my maternal grandmother during her last long years of life, after my grandfather died. My mother had memories of my grandmother that made it impossible for her to be sympathetic.

Blind in her old age, sitting outdoors when the weather was pleasant, my grandmother often heard my mother's movements when she was hanging clothes out on the line.

—¿*Eres tú, Dolores*? Is that you, Dolores?

My mother pretended not to hear and would not answer her. For the same reason—never having learned to read and write—she refused to let my father take us out of school to follow the crops, even when we were very poor and my father had difficulty finding work, because he was Mexican. For many years we were a family of eight, counting my mother and father, and it was difficult to make ends meet. Had it not been for my mother I would have been a migrant worker.

When my mother died, she left behind a trunk of memorabilia that has kept me busy for many years. She was amazingly systematic and organized, and she had a fabulous memory. I have countless cassette tapes of conversations that I recorded on my annual visits to Austin, from 1979 to 1985, with her and with my father. After she died, I videotaped the contents of the trunk that she left behind. For some strange reason, I did not cry at her funeral, but seeing in the contents of the trunk the remarkable woman that she was made me break down and I wept like a child. How ironic, I often thought, that I lived in a world of books, while she dwelled in a world of her own, a world of illiteracy. My mother, a woman who never learned to read and write, inspired a boy who went on to become a professor and a writer.

Many years later, when Dolores was outdoors during inclement weather, washing clothes by hand on one of those old washboards, or when she was ironing, cooking, and keeping house, she remembered her mother's words. In the hospital, Dolores Velásquez often thought of why she never learned to read and write. She remembered that day. ¡Escóndete, Dolores! Las mujeres no tienen que ir a la escuela.

XIV

THE GERMAN MAUSER

Natalie, our little girls, and I were visiting with my family on that Fourth of July years ago when drenching rains in Austin made the outdoor celebration of the U.S. Bicentennial impossible. In the next three years other visits confirmed the striking impression of that torrential visit. The elders in my family had entered an unusual period in their lives. I had discerned in them a heightened consciousness of getting old, which made me think in turn, that people of my generation were becoming elders too.

The rain storm kept us all indoors during the Fourth of July and other days of that summer visit. Consequently, the children, six and eight, played in one of the two guest rooms. In the evenings after they went to bed, Natalie and I spent many hours with my mother and father in the living room, sometimes quietly contemplative, watching their favorite telenovelas on the Mexican television station, listening to the rain on the roof and striking the windowpanes. The rain cleansed the summer air and made the earth smell rich and fertile. My father was full of memories and he told stories as if he could not help himself. My mother said that my father told the same stories over and over to anyone who would listen, to my brothers and my sister, for instance. She said that she knew them all by heart.

That year, after the rains stopped, Natalie and I took the children to Barton Springs with some of their little cousins. We also visited my father's two sisters, one in San Antonio, and they too, were immensely talkative and full of stories. I remember that in every conversation, whenever my aunts made mention of themselves and others, it was in a way that made me realize that like my mother and father they too were conscious of growing old.

They talked about people in the family and friends of the family who had died, how, when, and remembered how old they were. They told stories about people whom the dead had left behind, about their children and their grandchildren. They talked about the people who had come recently to wakes and funerals, about past anniversaries and approaching fiftieth wedding anniversaries, and about shared memories brought back just by looking into one another's faces at the funerals, remembering things that happened ten or fifteen or twenty years ago, or in some cases even thirty years ago. During our visit my mother and my aunts gave me many old photographs, fading and sepia colored, that were taken long ago with an old box camera. Giving me those photographs and other memorabilia, they talked about how important it is to pass on cherished objects and to keep them in the family.

In the following years I saw clearly from year to year not only an incremental consciousness of old age among the elders, I also saw them getting older. My father, then seventy-five, was determined even at that time, being remarkably strong and healthy for his age, to will himself to live until the age of one hundred ... *si Dios quiere* ... . God willing, he never fails to add. He speaks only Spanish at home, and very little English with a thick Mexican accent when he is working with people who do not know Spanish. In recent years, employing an American expression in Spanish with amusement and cheerfulness, he says also that of course, only if God does not back out on the promise that He made my father, or so my father says, just between the two of them. After all, my father said, had He wanted to call me, look at all the opportunities He had.

My father says that he wants to die working, pushing a lawnmower, pruning, and preferably stuck to a tree, he says with immense cheerfulness, and singing of course, like the *chicharra* in the Mexican song that sings until it dies leaving behind its dry shell stuck to a tree trunk or limb. He will be strong and healthy past ninety, and of a lucid mind until who knows when. He has told me stories about his childhood, about my grandfather, about his entire life, and about all those times when God had many opportunities to call him, had He wanted.

—I know that all of you will cry at my funeral, and that's fine. But don't get carried away with the tears. Just a few will be enough, just to let your heart breathe. Then bring on the mariachis and sing and dance to celebrate all the many years that God has granted so far to your mother and me, and all those still to come.

And there would be many years to follow. That year my father's sister, my *tía* Emily *la güera*, made a copy for me of her large photograph of my grandfather, after whom I was named. She would never part with the original, and I understand. It is a large oval portrait of head and shoulders that shows him down to the waist. In the photograph my grandfather is thirty-five years old. He is wearing the uniform of a cavalry soldier in the Mexican army. My copy of the photograph, now framed behind glass and enclosed in an oval mat, hangs on the wall of my study. It hangs alongside of photographs of my wife and our two daughters when they were babies, above a poster from some years ago of a Kathe Köllwitz exhibition at the Rioseco University Art Gallery, and these are all next to a large maple bookcase whose shelves are overloaded with books.

In the photograph my grandfather's black hair is cut short and combed neatly toward the back. His sideburns are trimmed high, which makes his well-shaped ears quite prominent. He wears a thin mustache, neatly trimmed, waxed and curled and pointed at the tips, like most Mexicans appear in photographs of the Mexican Revolution, in keeping with the custom of the time. Some people say that wearing the mustache in this manner was supposed to make Mexicans look more European, less Indian, because at the time even in Mexico there was discrimination against Indians and Mexicans whose skin was too dark.

On the left arm of his uniform jacket, as he stands turned just a little to the right, two stripes indicate his rank, a corporal. His jacket is buttoned all the way up to the neck. Above the collar of the jacket and below his chin a part of his shirt collar is visible. He stands almost solemnly at attention, shoulders back, chest out. There is a serious look on his face. His left eyebrow arches ever so slightly higher than the right, and between the two eyebrows are two pronounced vertical grooves, a physical trait which his sons, daughters, and some of his grandchildren have inherited from him.

In the left-hand pocket of his jacket is a small leatherbound notebook, one of many in which my grandfather kept a record of his experiences during the Mexican Revolution. He is wearing a cartridge belt around his waist.

Each time I look at this photograph of my grandfather it takes me back in memory to the last evening of our visit to Texas years ago. Natalie and the children were packing our suitcases. I was sitting in the living room with my mother and father. Suddenly my father stood up from his armchair when a commercial on the Mexican television station interrupted the telenovela we were watching. My mother, Natalie and I wondered what he was up to.

Without saying a word my father came and winked at me and at my mother, walked into the hallway and turning down the hall toward his and my mother's bedroom, he disappeared momentarily from sight. A few moments later he returned with a long object that was wrapped in towels. Carefully he began to remove the towels one at a time.

—What do you have there, Papa?

—*Un momentito,* he replied. Just wait and you will see.

A boyish, warm-hearted smile made his face joyfully radiant. After unwrapping several of the towels, my father shut his eyes firmly and then opened them, nodding his head as if in disbelief. Smiling, he was holding back tears brought to his eyes by proud filial memories. At last, he held a rifle in one hand and in the other some long, thin object that was still-wrapped in towels. He placed the still wrapped object on the sofa next to me, and now he held the rifle in his two hands as if it were a sacred object. My father was deeply moved. For what seemed like a long time he did not say a word, and neither my mother nor I spoke.

My father grasped the weapon at both ends of the stock, and he lifted and lowered the weapon gently, as if to get a sense of its weight. He turned the rifle one way and then another, looking at the weapon with what one could only regard as astonishment and disbelief. He pulled back the bolt to cock the hammer and then he depressed the empty magazine spring with his left thumb in order to return the bolt to its place. Now he brought the rifle up as if he were going to fire it. He placed the stock of the rifle firmly against his shoulder, took aim, and brought the rifle down three times, as if he were just practicing. He repeated his motions a fourth time, and now he aimed and squeezed the trigger gently and the hammer clicked.

—This weapon, my father said, with an emotion and pride that made him pause to catch his breath, is the rifle that your grandfather used when he was a cavalry soldier during the Mexican Revolution.

The bolt-action repeating rifle that my father was holding in his hands was no longer an ordinary weapon. Contemplating the effect of the weapon on her husband and son, my mother must have sensed it too. In my father's mind and in my own mind we must have sensed intuitively, that the rifle was the tangible extension of my grandfather's personality.

At that moment the rifle was more than just a rifle to the son and the grandson of the soldier; it was a concrete symbol in our hearts of the cavalry soldier's military courage and bearing, a repository of patriotic love of Mexico, a testament to his nationalism and its attendant antipathy, about which I had heard many times, for the gringo nation that stole more than half of Mexican territory in the war between the two countries. Undeniably, I thought, the rifle is a man-wrought instrument to kill other men. With it my grandfather had demonstrated his manliness many times over, and this object had outlived the man whose life it had watched over and protected. Over the years, however, removed from the context of bloody battles and violence, in the hearts of these two of his descendants, the rifle ceased to be a cold and deadly thing.

Memories of my grandfather in his old age, the passage of time, filial love and devotion, and the grandson's resemblance to the grandfather, all made the object something else. Its function was no longer to maim, pierce or wound the living flesh of other human beings, or to kill, though it still had that power. Now, in my father's gentle hands, it was harmless, a cherished object of veneration, a treasure inherited by my father, an object which ensured my grandfather's continuity in our memories. The rifle permitted the dead man to come and go among his living descendants because his soul and spirit inhabited the object that my father was holding and that he and I were contemplating.

The weapon stirred my father's heart and mine. The rifle made us conscious of my grandfather's presence in our blood. His obstinate blood seemed to be present in the genes and chromosomes that my father and I had inherited and had transmitted, each to his own children. My father, who regarded his father as a teacher of life, was assaulted by memories of his father that evening. In the years to come he would share countless memories with me.

My father looked at me that evening as if he were looking at his own father in the flesh, and my father's gaze and the love in his eyes made me imagine myself as my grandfather. I not only imagined my grandfather alive again in my own body, I felt his blood flowing in my veins. In that very living room, at that moment, the fact that I was named after him made the name itself something for me to cherish and take pride in, even more.

I have learned much more since that evening about my grandfather, and about my father's love for him. In telling stories about him my father gives to some people the impression that on account of old age and his son's devotion he is telling embellished stories. Now, looking back on that year, I see in retrospect a way of looking at death that I glimpsed when my brother Alejandro died, five years before that visit with my family, but which became understandable in my mind only years later, after another death, that of a dear friend who was also like a brother. The effect that the death of a loved one has on the living is connected with the way that the memory of the heart works.

Death sometimes works in strange ways. In the memory of the heart, traits of the dead person begin to acquire seemingly legendary dimensions, almost from the moment of death. When a person dies, a flood of memories rushes through one's mind, and simultaneously, many individual facets of the loved one's personality begin to coalesce in one's mind. A legend that develops around a person who has died is not necessarily exaggerated embellishment or distorted aggrandizement.

Legend may rightly be, it seems to me, only the enlarged and expanded consciousness, immediate and thereafter incremental, of countless remembered traits and qualities of a loved one, among them some that one may have taken for granted while the person lived. And this consciousness is attended by the realization that those traits were there all along. We had been carrying the remembrances within our hearts all the time, and it is death and the memory of the heart that make one conscious of cherished recollections and of a larger knowledge of a loved one. Death simply provokes our minds and hearts, it turns out, to recognize an accretion of memories, and

forces us to keep adding other traits to the posthumous mental portrait that the mind creates with remembered traits of the dead; and
this incremental remembering, involuntary and voluntary, natural
and inevitable, when guided by goodness and especially by love, leads
memory to dwell selectively on personal traits that are worthy of being preserved, and these worthy traits far surpass, one finds, disagreeable traits both big and small which trouble peoples' relationships in
life. The disagreeable traits of a person do not necessarily recede into
oblivion because they are less deserving of our hearts' remembrance.
And they loom large, of course, when grudges persist.

And we need not forget part of the truth either. We must tell the
good and the bad, yes, as my grandfather did in his notebooks. What
is desirable, however, is a rendering of a person's life, making an account with a generously good heart as a guide. Perhaps only the writer
wishes to remember disagreeable traits too, not to judge or to con-
demn, but to understand, for the writer recognizes the importance
of the whole picture of single human lives, whose importance in turn
sheds light on other pictures of many people's lives. Is that not why I
write, to understand, others and myself as well?

Several years do not diminish the vividness of my memory of the
effect that my grandfather's rifle was having on my father. In the
years that followed I asked my father about his childhood and adolescence, about what he remembered about Grandfather Miguel. And
he told me many stories. That evening, however, it was a privilege just
to watch my father during some eventful moments while he held and
turned the rifle over and over, feeling in his hands the weight of the
weapon with which my grandfather had killed many men when Mexico was at war with itself.

After what seemed a long while my father took a few steps toward
the sofa where I was sitting. He raised the rifle and placed the wood
stock in front of my eyes. He pointed to the initials on the wood
stock. M.V.-O. Miguel Velasquez-Ortiz. They had been crudely carved

into the wood with a knife. Below these letters was also the date 1911, the year when my grandfather joined the forces of Madero in Mexico City.

Then my father handed the rifle to me. In my hands the rifle seemed charged with an energy that it transferred to my whole body from some inexplicable and secret source. I had a similar experience when I became a father for the first time. When I used to hold my first infant daughter in my arms I could feel my own father's presence in my blood. Now, holding the rifle, what was going to be a prolonged and privileged state of spiritual rapture was interrupted temporarily by my mother's voice. A startled look had come upon her face, and she said that now I really looked like my grandfather. During that visit I began to learn much more about my family. Until then all that I had were my own memories of childhood and adolescence, which had not been privy to the memories of the elders.

My father told me that he had been saving the rifle for many years, until I was older and wiser. It was time for me to have it, he said. You are the eldest son of the generation that follows ours. You carry his name.

The weapon is, as I said, a bolt-action repeating rifle. It became one of my treasured possessions that year, along with the photographs that my mother and my aunts gave me. I took off my glasses in order to examine it closely. The rifle had the worn look of objects that have seen much use. The once beautiful hard wood of the stock and all the metal parts were dark and dulled by age. The muzzle, the whole action system, the trigger guard and trigger, the rear sight and the butt plate were of a dark raw umber. The metal parts were not rusty, however. One of the metal sling loops and the leather sling were missing. Thin lines of slightly oiled dirt crust had accumulated where the edges of the metal parts connected with the wood stock, and in the grooves of the screw heads.

ELIUD MARTÍNEZ   119

I paused and took a deep breath. I expelled the breath in a sigh. I saw, engraved on the upper metal part of the rifle the symbol of Mexico, an eagle atop a cactus and holding a serpent in its mouth. The symbol was at the front of the action, just outside the firing chamber, about two and a half inches behind the rear sight and in front of the magazine chamber. Above and curving around the symbol to form a half circle were engraved the words, REPUBLICA MEXICANA, in capital letters. Below the symbol was engraved the date when the weapon was manufactured, 1903, seven years before the Revolution started. On the left side of the magazine chamber was the name of the manufacturer in slightly smaller capital letters, DEUTCHE WAFFEN UND MUNITIONSFABRIKEN, and centered below this name in slightly larger capital letters, BERLIN. At the muzzle the edge of the wood stock was slightly chipped.

I stood up and said to my father that the rifle had been made in Germany. He said it was a Mauser rifle.

Holding the weapon at a slightly downward angle, with the wooden stock inside my right arm, I pulled the bolt back. The magazine and cartridge chambers were very dirty. I did not have to look down the muzzle to know that the barrel would also be unclean, that the rifling grooves would probably be impossible to see. It was in excellent condition, and with amusement I thought to myself that without a good cleaning it would not pass inspection. Then I tried to push the bolt back without success. It locked on me, I said to my father. No, my father said, you have to push down with your thumb, and he pointed to the spring lock of the cartridge chamber. When I depressed the spring the bolt went forward and in easily. The hammer was now cocked. If only this rifle could speak, I thought. What stories would it tell?

In handling the rifle I went through the same motions with it as had my father. I felt the weapon's weight in my hands. I turned it over and over, and then I brought the butt up to the hollow part of my shoulder, raising my right elbow high and my left elbow down under the weapon as I had been taught to handle an M-1 during military training. The butt of the rifle felt snug against the hollow part of my shoulder, against the deltoid muscle, which never forgets this particular contact with a similar object and tenses up by itself. Holding the weapon steadily I aimed at the small head of a nail on an empty space of wall. My finger was inside the trigger guard, against the trigger. My feet were slightly apart and firmly planted, instinctively ready for the impact of the weapon against my shoulder, which of course would not come from the unloaded rifle.

There is a name, a term, for that sudden backward thrust of the rifle against the shoulder when it is fired, but I cannot recall it. I remembered having been taught to squeeze the trigger slowly and gently, to avoid the shoulder's inclination to jerk in anticipation of that backward thrust and to avoid closing one's eyes before the weapon fires. I began to squeeze the trigger very slowly.

The head of the nail was just slightly above the front sight of the rifle. My mother and father and I did not say a word. This time I fell into a prolonged trance. In my mind the space of wall surrounding the nail became a picture screen. Scenes of my young manhood during the time of my military service passed through my mind. I became the warrior trained to kill. The weapon in my hands brought back scenes of the Mexican Revolution about which I had read in novels, which I had seen in films, and which were the subject of revolutionary *corridos*, those wonderful ballads that were composed by itinerant poets to commemorate major battles and great heroes and simple soldiers and the women who followed them, the *guerrilleras*. These were the songs which the people would sing by the camp fire at the end of the day. Many were songs that I had heard since I was a child. I remembered almost fabled names of cities where important battles took place: Zacatecas, Ciudad Victoria, Laredo, Torreon, Celaya, Hermosillo, and many others. Then I felt myself transported through time, and a series of images began to pass in front of my astonished eyes. The images passed in rapid-fire succession and assaulted my senses.

The front and rear sights of my grandfather's German Mauser were aligned and I aimed at imaginary targets. Before my very eyes the shapes of men and horses, of women and children, began to take form beyond the peak of the rifle's front sight. I saw things that I have seen in numerous documentary photographs of the Revolution: great throngs of people dashing for cover behind massive colonial buildings, behind rocks and boulders; hiding in hills and mountains or behind the trunks of trees; scurrying out of sight behind bushes; firing from the arched entranceways of colonial buildings and from rooftops, behind crenellations and polichromed tile domes and towers; I saw men on horseback firing pistols and imagined hearing them giving orders and cursing ... *dáles en la madre a los jijos de la tiznada ...¡Tóma cabrones pa que sepan quien son los meros chingones!* I heard the loud reports of pistols and rifles, the thunder of cannons; I heard the screams of women and children and saw them scattered by singing bullets; I heard the thunderous hoofbeats of charging horses; I saw anonymous men fall from horses and rooftops, men running and horses with empty saddles galloping across great empty plazas and narrow streets, men and horses felled by bullets fired from trenches or from rooftops; I saw bodies of the dead strewn across one another in the middle of streets and plazas, and the blood oozing out of their bodies from holes in the chest and from gaping empty eye-sockets; I saw dead men smeared with blood and dirt, trampled by horrified horses; I heard the sounds of rifles smashing human flesh and bone; I saw corpses that had been dismembered by sabers and cannon fire, over there an arm or a hand far from the body of which it had been a part, and beyond, a head or a leg which had been severed in some way from the still-warm corpses; I saw men ripping away the clothing of girls and women, and the women's helpless wild rolling eyes as they were being violated; I heard the cries of helpless women pleading for mercy; I saw men running out of churches clutching gold and silver icons and candlestick holders; I heard the murmuring of prayers, the invocations to God; I saw fear inscribed on the faces of simple men with great mustaches and large sombreros, of men who knew not the political ideas that divided Mexicans into warring factions, of men who had not the faintest knowledge of the ideologies that drove some men to hunger for power and fame and that impelled others toward honorable causes; I imagined the smell of gun powder and the stench of rotting corpses; dust and smoke filling my nostrils.

I saw anonymous men with large sombreros, wearing *guaraches* and dirty white peasant clothing, passing across the sights of my grand-father's rifle, some safely, others stopped dead in the tracks by soldiers' bullets that found their mark; and I saw still more anonymous men dashing for cover across still more narrow streets, and others on horseback charging after them; I saw the glint of sunlight on upraised sabers, and I heard harsh mighty voices barking orders and hurling curses and the obedient *sí, mi capitán* or *sí, mi general*, which the wind made faint as it carried the voices away; I saw many more bleeding bodies of anonymous men, strewn on the dirt ground of villages; I saw fear on faces of men who were about to die; I saw on countless anonymous faces valor and cowardice, the animal lust for women, the reprehensible drive toward power, great dignity and pride, confusion and horror, brute ecstasy and bewilderment. All this my grandfather must have seen, I thought. I imagined the dangers that he must have faced. Ahead of these sights, perhaps a soldier had taken aim at my grandfather. It may be that my grandfather shot first.

Experienced warrior and trained to kill, I squeezed the trigger slowly, gently. I imagined a face. The thought of shattering and splintering the bone of the enemy's face did not make me cringe with revulsion. Slowly I squeezed until the hammer of the German Mauser clicked. When it did so I emerged from the enraptured state of mind and found myself in the living room of my parents' home, still aiming at the head of a nail on an empty wall.

Many years have passed since my father gave me my grandfather's rifle. Since then I have learned much more about the miraculous powers of memory. Today, I see that the rifle is a repository of memories. When I hold it in my hands now I remember all those scenes which I have described, that I can see not only with my own inward eyes, but also with my grandfather's eyes at a second remove, with the eyes of my father at still a third remove, and with the eyes of memory. It may be that the three whiskeys which I had consumed earlier that evening also contributed to the unusual effect of the rifle that made my inward vision visible.

After all, I was holding an object that my grandfather had held, against which he had pressed the warmth of his living hands. The wood stock of the rifle had soaked in and retained the sweat of his hands. Particles of his skin had merged with linseed and machine oil and dirt to form little crusty ridges. The sudden convergence in my mind of countless scenes, voices, sounds and other sensory impressions, and of my knowledge of the Mexican Revolution gleaned from novels, films and *corridos*, had occurred, simply I think, because of the magic that inheres in old and used objects that become inherited family heirlooms, especially when one loves the person whose personal possession it had been, and when one cherishes the memories of that person, which an object, like songs from the past, frees involuntarily from the storehouse of memory.

In the following years my father, my aunts and my mother would tell me many stories about my grandfather, without their being always in agreement, for the memory of their respective hearts remembers things differently, and these stories too, now converge upon my mind when I hold the rifle in my hands, pull back the bolt, depress the magazine spring, push back the bolt, raise the rifle, aim and squeeze the trigger. Mine was an experience akin to dreaming, and to this day I regard the experience as a privileged one not usually allowed the waking mind.

A few moments later, on that same evening when my father gave me the rifle, he also gave me something else. He picked up the other long thin object wrapped in towels that he had placed on the sofa next to where I was sitting, and while I was handling the rifle he had unwrapped it. It was my grandfather's cavalry saber, still in its steel sheath. My mother was looking at the two of us through the thick lenses of her glasses. She was amused with the two of us, and pleased I thought then, but three or four years later I would learn otherwise. For her, the memories of my grandfather that the two objects evoked were not pleasant.

Three times my father slipped the saber up and down in its sheath without withdrawing it. Each time the handguard struck against the metal opening of the sheath with a loud clunking noise that was pleasing to my ears. Then he withdrew the saber all the way out. As the sharp point of the saber emerged from the sheath the sound of steel rubbing against steel seemed to linger momentarily in the air. He extended his arm forward, holding the saber as if he were giving the command to charge. The blade, almost a yard long, curved down and upward toward a sharp point. Then my father bent his elbow and brought the thick edge of the blade to rest against his right shoulder, like a rifle at arms.

¡Chingao! my father exclaimed, unable to contain his laughter. He said that when he was a youngster he used to see his father turn men into cowards with the saber. He said that after his father came back from the Revolution, when men wanted to fight him, he would instill fear in other men because he would fight only to the death. If a man were unarmed, my father said, my grandfather would simply chase him away with the saber. Sometimes, my father said cheerfully, he would get in a good lick with the side of the blade against the buttocks or the legs before they got away.

—He took me with him everywhere he went. He knew that I would always look after him if he drank too much. Many times, in his cups, he would try to start a fight, and I would have to pull him away and take him home, sometimes on my back. The older men would understand and let me take him away. I was a very strong boy, stronger than some grown men. I was the only one that he would listen to ... *era bárbaro mi papa* ... . If I had not pulled him away from some of those situations he would never have lived as long as he did. Someone would have killed him eventually. He was afraid of no man, sober or drunk. There is your brother Andrés. My father was no taller than Andrés, five-five perhaps, but like your brother, he had powerful arms, shoulders, and a broad back. Sometimes when I look at your brother, especially his habits, I tell myself, there is my father all over again. *¿Verdá Dolores?*

My mother pretended not to hear. My father returned the saber to its sheath, and I exchanged the rifle for the saber. The sheath was dark. Here and there was some rust. The bronze hand guard of the saber's grip, which protects the hand knuckles against other sabers in hand-to-hand combat, was of a simple and functional design. Without adornment the simple hand guard reminded me of the flowing lines of art nouveau. A dark film had formed on it and protected this durable metal alloy from corrosion. In close combat the hand guard can probably serve as brass knuckles too, I thought. I looked at the grip itself closely. The wood was almost completely exposed. Only a little amount remained of the strong leather-covered thin chord with which the handle had once been wrapped. It was hard to tell if the leather had been a dark brown or maroon color. In places the leather had been completely worn away, exposing the chord. The spaces formed by the narrow bands of the leather-covered chord were once decorated with a very thin shiny gold thread that also went around the handle. Only four thin lines of this decorative thread remained near the tip of the hand guard. I slipped the saber out of its sheath.

I imagined what it must have looked like when it was new and bright and shining. The singled edge blade was dark with age, but not rusty. My father told me that my grandfather had explained the shape and function of the saber. The blade curves down and up so that when it is thrust into a person's body—and he pointed to the place where the rib cage meets below the sternum—it will go up and reach the heart behind the rib cage. Pointing to the sides of the blade he said that the recessed parts were called blood grooves, and that these permitted the withdrawal of the blade from human flesh. Otherwise the flesh would grip the inserted blade tightly and make it difficult to withdraw. The blood grooves enable the blade to ride out smoothly on the flow of blood, my father said.

When I extended my arm with the saber in my hand I could not help but think of it as a protective extension of a man's arm. Far, far back in history, I reflected, man had discovered weapons, as he had discovered fire and agriculture and the wheel, in the beginning perhaps mainly to protect himself from great predatory animals and from his enemies. On the way to becoming a full-fledged biped he had learned to kill, and eventually he would learn that the extension of his arms would give him added courage and power, and that having once killed, he could kill again, and eventually in man there would develop a lust to power and a will to conquer and dominate other men. In a single short sequence of a film one filmmaker had compressed thousands of years of weapon development by man.

The scene is taken with the camera placed low, very close to the ground. In the scene, shot in slow motion, a prehistoric man, clad only in a loin cloth made with the skin of an animal, is crouching. Towering above the camera, he is in the middle of the frame. The picture composition and the low angle of the shot are immensely impressive on a huge picture screen. In front of him is the skeletal rib cage of a large animal. The curved bones rise up and around from a pile of other bones. The man reaches out and grasps a large, long bone in his hand. Very slowly and in total silence, if memory serves me correctly, holding the bone the man extends his arm. Several times he taps the other bones, gently, with the end of the bone as if he were using a hammer. Several times, in slow motion, he raises his arm and he brings the bone down on the skeleton, each time with increasing force. In the man's eyes one can read the very process of a discovery that leads to a moment of illumination. At last the man raises his arm very high, bringing himself up to an almost standing position, and with a terrible force the man brings the weight of his own body to bear on the arm and the bone which comes crashing down on the animal skeleton. The crashing blow raises dust and shatters pieces of bones that scatter in the air, in slow motion. The eyes of the man now shine wildly with a new knowledge. Brute ecstasy is written on his face. He turns now one way and then another. Incredulity wars on his face with the reality he has just witnessed. And no other question can possibly be passing through his mind except, why had he never before thought of using a large bone in this way, as a club?

Our human ancestor is delirious with the joy of having discovered a weapon, an extension of his arm. He has discovered power over predatory animals, a power that he will subsequently use against other beings like himself. In the centuries to come man will decorate his bone weapons; and centuries later, as the film illustrates, man will discover ways of making weapons with iron and bronze, which he will also decorate. He will learn in the centuries to follow how to make knives and spears, and still more centuries later, he will learn to make even more sophisticated weapons with which to kill and conquer and rule. Still centuries later, men from the Mediterranean will arrive on our continent with flaming weapons and swords and horses, and they will clash in bloody battles and mingle their blood and culture with those of the inhabitants, to produce the nation for which people like my grandfather fought, on horseback and on foot; and my grandfather will use weapons more advanced slightly than those of the Mediterraneans from whom we are also descended. In the decades to come human beings will know more refined instruments, which by this time men and women will learn to use to kill others.

I reflected some more. My grandfather's saber, by way of a remarkable film, had transported me back in my imagination to the discovery by one of our ancestors of the first club, a bone weapon. I shared my thoughts with my mother and father. The saber reminded me, I told them, that long ago men used the bones of animals as clubs and that it took thousands and thousands of years for them to discover spears and bows and arrows and gun powder and rifles and cannons and atom bombs. They laughed at my wild imagination, and my father said to my mother that what she was seeing is what happens to a person when he reads too many books. *Se ha vuelto loco*, he said. We laughed together, warmly. I thought about my grandfather and my head filled with romantic notions about the magic of heredity. At that moment I felt in my heart, now that the rifle and saber were mine, that the spirit of my grandfather had become one with my own.

XV

MY GRANDFATHER'S HORSE

Standing by his car José asked Miguel's father if he had been born in Mexico.

—*Sí*, the old man answered simply.

This response was a simple straightforward yes. But when José asked the old man when he came to the United States, a faraway look came into the old man's eyes and a rapturous expression spread itself across the old man's face.

—*¿Cuándo vino usted a los Estados Unidos?*

The second question prompted a moment of silence. In that moment the old man began, in his mind's eye, to make a sweeping survey of his life. The question was an invitation to review the spectacle of his remarkable life. Miguel knew from the familiar, thoughtful look on his father's face that the question had set in motion a memory voyage.

Miguel's friend José could not help but also notice the look on the face of the old man. By this time Miguel knew that in his father's memories weighty chronology prevails. Between the two questions, Antonio's memory had taken flight, back to the year of his birth and forward from there to his ninth year. In the special glow of his father's eyes Miguel could see that the old man's memory had begun to work, silently at first. José, too, was struck by the rapturous glow, as if at the back of the eyes some unusual source of light illuminated each retina. The old man seemed to have entered into a trance-like state. When he began to speak, his voice seemed to come from far away. The old man's speech was slow and measured. He chose his words carefully. Miguel and José listened.

One could visualize the old man's memory at work. Effortlessly his memory was selecting from among countless images and multiple alternative beginnings for the story he was about to tell. After talking a little about himself he inevitably remembered his own father. Once into the story Antonio's memory brought forth the exact words that were spoken many years ago, by whom, under what circumstances, where, at what time of day or night, and who were the people whose words he was repeating, and what had brought so many men together, fifty of them. Many of them, he said—*eran padres de más de cuatro*—were fathers with more than four children at that, but they agreed to go with my father to join Francisco Madero and to fight in the Revolution.

The image of Antonio's father took shape and substance in the old man's words. With astonishing ease the octogenarian storyteller reviewed the memories of long ago, of when his father went off to the Revolution, and he recalled stories that he had heard directly from his father after he returned, and that as a child he read in the notebooks that the revolutionary cavalry soldier had kept of his experiences.

His fabulous memory reviewed, selected, and arranged the dialogue and the details of setting and time, the names of the principal protagonists of the story. Each word and phrase seemed to give natural birth to other words and phrases. José and Miguel witnessed the orderly proliferation of amazingly remembered details in an illuminated elderly mind. The memories expanded like circles in water into which a stone has been cast. The words multiplied the roles that the elderly Antonio had played in life. Dutiful son and father too, husband, brother, friend, and more. The old man held the two younger men captive. His storytelling cast a spell upon them.

There was a basic storyline. After making a few prefatory comments Antonio told about the night when his father had gone from one cantina to another to recruit men to go and join Francisco I. Madero in his effort to remove the tyrant Porfirio Díaz. Miguel's father selected an historical event that had affected the entire direction of his own life in the United States, to respond to José's question, to tell José that Miguel's grandfather had entered the United States with his family a few years before the Revolution, he could not remember exactly when, because Antonio was but a child. At the time, along with himself, he had a brother and two sisters who were also born in Cerralvo, Nuevo Leon. All the other brothers and sisters were born in Texas, he said, in the area of McAllen, Darwin, and Laredo. All this the old man narrated briefly. His memory was going elsewhere, on to something much more important, and the manner in which he was to tell the main story evinced the gifts of a natural-born storyteller.

Miguel's father told a story that he may have told many times before, one that in following years he would tell again, more than once. On November 20, 1910, when the Revolution erupted, he said, he was nine years old, attending a little village school across the border, in Colombia, Nuevo León. In the weeks and months after the Revolution started it was reported in all the newspapers. People were talking about it. There was fighting in some of the border towns and in the north of Mexico. On the Texas side of the border we could hear cannon fire, rifles shooting, he said, and we could see buildings going up in flames.

—One night, early in the year 1911, my father went from cantina to cantina. He recruited fifty men, some who had already had a lot to drink, and the next morning, very early, they left, on horseback. I saw my father on his horse. He waved and told me to look after my mother and my little brothers and sisters, until he returned. *Cuídalos, Antonio, hasta que yo regrese.*

Miguel's father then described in great detail the journey into the interior, as his father had told him or written it down in one of his notebooks, the reception in Mexico City by Francisco I. Madero himself. Then he told his father's story about an untamed horse that no one but his father could ride.

As he spoke, Antonio would change the inflection of his voice to indicate a change of speaker in a dialogue. The old man was marvelous at imitating the bold language of his father, the speech of soldiers and generals, the language of patriotic nationalism. He succeeded in conjuring up voices and the protagonists of his story.

Miguel and José listened with delightful admiration. Later José told Miguel that his father was a natural-born storyteller.

—Did you notice, Miguel, how your father narrates parts of the story in his own voice? How he changes his voice when within his story another person speaks, with minimal directions in the manner of a playwright? You can almost hear and see the actors on a stage. In telling the story your father was playing many parts. His memory of details is fantastic. It would take a highly gifted writer with a good ear for the conversational quality of spoken language to render your father's stories in his own words. Your father reminds me of don Lucas in *Al filo del agua*. He brings to mind many of Rulfo's stories. Some of our own Chicano writers have succeeded in rendering something of the flavor of our spoken language which we find among the elders. It's a part of our linguistic heritage that more of our writers should preserve.

Several years later, when Miguel is visiting in Austin, his father will tell the same story. This time Miguel will make notes. Knowing that one day he will write the story in English, he resigned himself to the fact that the flavor of his father's sixteenth century Spanish language could never be satisfactorily rendered in English.

Few things during the past two decades delighted the elderly Antonio more than to talk about his father Miguel Velásquez, the cavalry soldier. And the stories about him also delighted the grandson. His father cherished the memories of his father, and even though he was an old man speaking, his voice and the feelings expressed were not the voice and feelings of an old man. The words that he spoke came from deep within, from the child that still resided in him.

The octogenarian always spoke, regardless of his age, with the true veneration of a child for the father. Miguel loves his father's *norteño* language. Many of the words his father uses can be traced back to the Castilian language of the sixteenth and seventeenth centuries, preserved amazingly among northern Mexicans, particularly among those who did not have the opportunity to attend the university and who transmit this spoken language from generation to generation.

Unfortunately for the grandson, he studied at the Universidad Autónoma de México, where university Spanish took precedence in his educated mind over the rich language that he heard at home when he was a child. Miguel regretted sometimes that attending the university had placed his father's language beyond his reach.

One day during that visit, responding to his son Miguel's wanting to know about his grandfather's notebooks, his father, now close to being ninety years old, spoke about his father in beautiful *norteño* Spanish.

—In his notebooks my father wrote everything down, hijo. Good or bad, he would write it down. *Hay que decir la pura verdá, lo bueno con lo malo,* he used to say, *a calzón quitao.* He believed that the truth had to be told, regardless of what people might say. I remember that my mother was shocked by some of the things he wrote. *¡Ay hombre! ¿Cómo te pones a escribir tales cosas?* How he could write such things? But my father would say that the truth is the truth. I remember that whatever he wrote was very detailed. But my memory is not what it used to be. *Hace muchos años, hijo.* It was a long time ago. All I have left are impressions about very detailed entries in his notebooks, about his experiences, and about his handwriting. It was very elegant.

—Can you give me some general examples of details, Papá?

—*Sí, hijo.* I read in his notebooks how he would get on his horse, for example. How he would talk to the horse, and how the animal trusted my father. Man and horse were very close in those days. A man's life very often depended on mutual trust with his horse, my father said. He wrote about how he got the horse to listen and to obey. He described his affection for the horse. Oh! My father was a horseman, *¡sí señor!* He was one of the best.

I remember reading in my father's notebooks about the orders that the military leaders gave to the troops. Some orders were spoken, and those who received them would say, *sí mi general, sí mi teniente,* and so on. Other orders were transmitted by the trumpet. Your grandfather wrote that the trumpet awakened the troops in the early morning. The orders to mount, to march, to halt, to attack, to retreat were given with a trumpet. In my imagination I could see the soldiers as if I were there myself, waking up in the morning, being called to formation, being inspected, preparing for the journey, on horseback, or on a train. He described the orders to prepare for mounting the horses, to march. All-l-l-right-t moun-n-nt-t! Hand-d-ds-s on the saber-r-r! and so on.

Even the horses knew the orders. Can you imagine? A trumpet! *¡Híjole!* Even though I never rode a horse in my life, when I would read his notebooks they made me feel like I was on a horse. His notebooks made me choke on the dust raised by the horses' hoofs when they were passing over dry plains and dusty lands. It would get into the hairs in your nose, he wrote. *Sí, m'hijo,* he was a good writer. Such a shame what happened to the notebooks of my father. Imagine what you could have done with them, with your university education. You could have published them, in *castellano* and in English. Two languages! *¡Chingao!* What a loss! Such a tragedy that they were destroyed, by that goat! It came into the house when we were all on a picnic ... .

—A goat? Did you say another time that it was a burro? Or, maybe it was *tía* Celia who said it was a burro. In any case she said it was a lovable pet animal.

—No, no. I am pretty sure it was a goat.

Anyway, he was a good writer, my father. He wrote about the people who greeted them when they arrived at small towns and villages. He described the way that the horses smelled after a long day's journey, the way the men and the women smelled when they did not take a bath for days. He wrote everything. If they stopped to urinate or to do something else, he wrote that down. He wrote about the brief stops at towns and villages, negotiating with people about food and sleeping quarters.

In one of the notebooks he wrote about coming to a village from which all the men, except for those who were very old, were gone. They used to force the young men to join them. When the young men knew soldiers were coming they fled and they would hide their young women and girls. But in one village there were many girls, he wrote, between thirteen and sixteen years old. They were women already. Some women had dreams of leaving the place where they were born. So when the soldiers left, some of the girls followed the soldiers.

My father also wrote about long journeys by train. The trains carried men, horses, heavy weapons over long distances between towns, because otherwise the horses would get very tired. After every battle, at night before going to sleep, he would write about it. He got to know the whole country during the Revolution, on trains and on horseback, too. My father must have known every city and river and mountain in Mexico, and by name too. And to think that he did not know how to read and write until after he married my mother! Ah! But that is another story.

You asked me to tell you about the notebooks. What else do you want me to tell you? You should ask my sisters too. They also remember him. They remember things that I have forgotten. I need someone who remembers the same things in order to remember what I have forgotten. When we talk, then I can remember. Like sometimes, when I listen to *corridos* about battles and places during the Revolution, I remember my father. I think about his notebooks. *¡Chingao!* I say to myself. My father was probably there, or I wonder if he was there. He knew so much. He taught me many things. I remember him all the time. But my memory is not as good as it used to be.

You know, hijo. Just like my memory, my body is going. A little at a time. My hands refuse to obey me. Look at this thumb. And my legs hurt sometimes. My hands will no longer do my bidding. If I sit down to watch television for half an hour I can barely stand. I used to spring up from a sitting position like a cat. Like a cat! Not anymore. But it's amazing, when I am working nothing hurts me. I feel like I did when I was fifty. Anyway, it is getting late. Your mother and I are sleepy. We can continue our conversation tomorrow. *¿Verdá? No mentira, hijo. ¿Dolores, nos vamos a acostar ya?*

—What a miracle, she said. He got tired of talking! He wants to go to sleep. Who would have believed it?

These few details about the story that his father began to tell him reminded Miguel that his father may have told him this story seven or eight years ago. He listened without saying a word, outlining briefly the gist of the story, thinking there will be plenty of time to write it up. He recalled his father's words.

The next evening, his memory now at home in the distant past, the elderly father said to his eldest son that he wanted to tell him a story. Come to the kitchen, so we don't disturb your mother while she's watching television. *Ven, hijo.* And his son followed him into the kitchen, where they each took a chair at the table and sat down.

—I remember when my father went off to the revolution, with fifty men, most of them fathers of large families, with more than four children. I was just nine years old when the Revolution broke out. Almost ten, but not quite. Fifty men went with him. He made the rounds of the cantinas one night, just a few weeks after the Revolution started.

By 1911 my father had already heard about Francisco Madero, and being favorably disposed to help in toppling the old dictator Porfirio Díaz, he went one night from one cantina to the next, speaking to men willing to go with him. The next morning they all went with my father and crossed the border from Texas into the border town of Colombia.

I was attending school in Colombia at the time, and my teacher had come to speak with my father about sending me to study in Monterrey. I have told you about Maestro Cabral before. Well, as I was saying, these fifty men and my father crossed the Río Bravo (in those days it was not called the Río Grande), and in Colombia my father went directly to General Naranjo.

I cannot remember his first name, but he and my father were friends since they were boys, and the general asked my father how he could be of help. What do your men need? And my father said, We need horses to get to the capital, so we can help don Francisco Madero topple don Porfirio from the presidency. And not only was General Naranjo a friend of my father, but he, too, supported Madero and wanted don Porfirio removed from office. Well, so he gave all fifty men and my father horses and they all went to Mexico City, and there in the capital, my father went directly to don Francisco Madero to pledge their support, and this was just shortly after don Francisco had been declared the President of Mexico.

—*Señor Presidente Madero*, it is an honor to meet you. I am Miguel Velásquez, and I come with fifty men who love Mexico very much, all the way from Texas, and we are all ready to assist you and to obey your orders. We are all *norteños*.

After my grandfather learned how to read and write he spoke more diplomatically, my father said.

Learning that they were *norteños* like himself, President Madero was additionally pleased that my father and the fifty men had come from the north to pledge their support.

—And what are the needs of your men, Señor Velásquez?

My father told don Francisco that they needed good horses because those that General Naranjo had given them were exhausted and weakened by the long journey. The President also asked them other questions.

—Do you and your men know how to read and write?

—Some of us do, a little, and some of us do not, my father responded.

Then the President asked my father if he and his men knew anything about being soldiers. My father told him that some knew a little, but that the majority were just simple men. But everyone is ready to follow you and to obey whatever you command, *señor Presidente.* The President was astonished.

El Presidente Madero se quedó asombrado.

—*¿Qué más necesitan?*

—*Armas.* That's what we need. Where do we obtain arms?

Then the President gave orders that the men and my father each be given a good horse, a saddle, a pistol, cartridge belts, plenty of cartridges, and a Mauser rifle. Among the horses there was one that my father liked, a black and white horse.

At first the man who took care of the horses did not want to give it to my father.

—No, he said to my father, this horse is very dangerous. It is too wild and it kicks. It could kill a man.

But my father insisted, and when the man still refused, my father went directly to the President and talked to him about the horse. He spoke very politely to President Madero.

—*Mi Presidente, mire usted* ... Look, sir, there is a black and white horse that I like very much. The sergeant in charge of the horses tells me that the horse is dangerous and capable of killing a man. He says no man can put a saddle on this horse, much less ride him. That is the horse that pleases me the most, and I would like to request respectfully that you not blame the sergeant if anything happens to me for trying to saddle and ride him. He has already warned me about the horse, but I like the horse very much.

Well, hijo, my father got the horse. Anyway, he always carried little sugar cubes with him, and a little bottle of whiskey. He knew that horses like sugar. He got close to the horse, spoke very softly to it, gave it a cube of sugar dipped in whiskey, and the horse like it. So the horse brought its head next to my father as if asking for more, and my father gave the horse another sugar cube dipped in whiskey, and all the time speaking with the horse very gently, very softly and affectionately. Little by little my father gained the horse's trust. Meanwhile, all the men who came with him from Texas, and the sergeant who was in charge of the horses, were watching my father talking very calmly and softly to the horse.

—*Bueno, caballito.* Now I am going to put the saddle on your back. The horse did not move. All the men were astonished to see the horse not budge when the saddle went on its back, and more so when my father mounted the horse. After that they were given their Mauser rifles, but whenever the sergeant or anyone came near the horse it would rear up on its hind legs, snort and rend the air with its neighing.

Everyone was afraid of the horse. Only my father could control it, and this black and white horse turned out to be my father's very best horse. It could jump, and it never got tired. It obeyed my father. The black and white horse was a fast runner, too. Finally, one day the Zapatistas shot it in the belly and killed it when the horse jumped over their trench. Fortunately, my father fell from the dead horse and was not hurt.

Later on my father had another good horse, and this is the horse that he rode on all the way back to Texas, when he was released from military service, in Cuernavaca, right after that nefarious Victoriano Huerta ordered the assassination of don Francisco Madero and his Vice-Presidente. *¡Híjole, hijo,* what an intelligent horse that first one was, the black and white one! And the second one too, so much so that the *rinches* wanted to take it away from my father, because he refused to sell the horse to them, and several men wanted to buy it from him, and then one day he did sell it, but to a *mexicano.*

The second horse had a name, too, but I cannot remember it anymore. My memory is not what it used to be. Wait, I think it got its name from the twig of a tree – the second horse that my father brought all the way from Cuernavaca was slim and swift – yes, like the twig of a limb from a tree. *Varañitas* was the name of my father's horse. Yes, hijo, I think so, but my memory is not what it used to be.

XVI

SE VENDE MULATA BLANCA: WHITE MULATTA FOR SALE

Miguel Velásquez opened the pocket notebook that he took with him to Texas to the first undated page. He had been there a little more than a month ago. He wondered when he had made the list of those film titles. The films had one thing in common. They explored varieties of the theme of love.

At the top of the list was *Camila*, based on a true story of forbidden love involving a young Jesuit priest and a young woman, daughter of a wealthy aristocrat in mid-nineteenth century Buenos Aires. The film reminded him of Abélard and Héloïse. Abélard was also a man of the church, thirty-seven years old, and Héloïse seventeen when she became his student. One can easily imagine the young, beautiful and brilliant Héloïse with her teacher Abélard, the two of them sitting side by side at a table, on a regular basis, in front of an open book, in a cool monastery cell, in his study, among many shelves of books.

Miguel imagined the attraction felt by the girl—a young woman better still—for the bright mind of the man who was a theologian, poet, and teacher, and later, for the man who became her lover, the father of her child. One can imagine her glancing away from the pages of the book from time to time, holding one finger over the place on the passage he has asked her to analyze. Use logic, he said to her, and now turning her beautiful face ever so slightly to gaze into his eyes she is warmly conscious that they are sitting so close that they can each feel the warmth of the other's body. A man of thirty-seven and a young woman of seventeen.

After bearing his child they married, but Héloïse's uncle, a fellow canon of Abélard at the École de la Cathédral de Notre Dame, forced them to separate, and he hired some evil, brutal men to attack Abélard and to deprive him of his sexual virility. Héloïse became a nun, and from her convent she wrote to him a series of love letters, among the most beautiful, tender, and passionate ever written, in which she employed intellectual skills and logical analysis, superior to his it has been written, to celebrate their joyous, joyous love, their intense and magical May-September ephemeral love which ended with his tragic calamity and with her in a convent.

Looking away from the pocket notebook and examining his trembling soul with his mind's eye, Miguel wondered. Was it worth the price to have known such exquisite, forbidden, ephemeral love? For Abélard yes, it was worth it. Miguel knew that in the days to come he would go back and read again the letters of Héloïse to Peter Abélard.

Next on his list was *Ruby Gentry*, by King Vidor, the first film of tragic love that so deeply troubled him when he first saw the film, and which he had been trying to find for years without success. He was very young when he saw the film, and his heart knew for the first time the wildness of rapture and passion that made him weep. He wept too because at the end of the film the beautiful Jennifer Jones, the Ruby of the film, dies.

In all the years of his life to follow he would never put out of his mind the unforgettable image of Jennifer Jones' beautiful, young undulant form. Several times during the film, the same image of her young and exquisite body fills the screen. Magnificently seductive and vibrantly alive with sexual energy, framed by the door to the shack of her poor white family, she is silhouetted from behind by the light of a kerosene lamp that illuminates the shack ... Ruby! ... *Ruby-y-y* ... *you're like a song-g-g* ... *you don't know right from wrong* ... . Oh, young

Jennifer Jones ... .

He would never forget that image, nor would he forget the inexplicable, the breathtaking desire for that silhouetted form framed by the door, the longing that clamored in his loins; and now he remembered also the beautiful hills and gently flowing valleys of her reclining body at the end of the film, after Charleton Heston and Jennifer Jones shot and killed each other, when they die in each others' arms. Dead, beautiful, exquisite Jennifer Jones.

No, he would never forget the intensity of his longing to get up from his seat in the Paramount Theatre in Austin, and to walk into the screen and to hold her, weeping, his eyes flooded with tears, and that is how he ran out of the theater after seeing the very first film with a tragic ending, and for the rest of his life he would remember that first association of death and making love that gives to the erotic impulse an added, strangely bizarre *frisson*.

In years to come, he would remember Ruby, he would remember Jennifer Jones, and one day he would ask himself whether this lust had been necrophilia. He would realize years later, because then, despite his age, he did not yet make a distinction between the actress and the character of the film, that he had actually longed to hold the dead Ruby Gentry in his arms, and there was nothing that he could do about the desire.

He would remember in years to come that he felt it, deeply, passionately, unforgettably, and that he had yielded to desire. Ruby! Jennifer! What did it matter? A woman, an actress, a character in a movie had made him long for fever, for passion. His life was never to be the same after that.

He graduated from high school and enrolled at the university. In November, a married woman six years older than he would carry him gently across the bridge into the land of manhood. That, too, he would remember for the rest of his life. And after that, each time he saw her he would make her laugh because he would always tell her that she was the first woman in his life ... *tú eres la primera mujer en mi vida, y jamás te olvidaré.*

He ran his finger across several film titles, and at the bottom of the list his finger went from left to right, across Carlos Saura's *El amor brujo.* How could one translate such a title, one that conjured up sorcery, magic, enchantment? *Bewitching Love.* Words are so helpless sometimes when one has to translate from one language to another, when words embody custom, culture, superstition, and bewitching love.

What is *amor brujo?* It is the love of gypsies, of nocturnal wanderers, of carnival people, of actors and actresses. It is magical love. It is mystical, ephemeral love. And so it is in Saura's film. *Amor brujo* is love that comes from the afterlife, from another world. The words speak of love that comes to the lover with dim, vague memories of having lived in another time and place. The film is about memories of having been lovers somewhere in time. The memories speak. The title of Saura's film reminded him that on the night when he first saw the film, he had a dream.

In his dream a wise woman's voice spoke as if it were coming from a great distance ... . *Hace casí ciento cuarenta años* ... she was speaking to her daughter in Spanish .... "Nearly one hundred and forty years ago a mother like me spoke to her blossoming daughter who was just like you. Their home was located on the plains of northern Mexico. Their people had wandered north, away from the Gulf of Mexico, from the coast of Vera Cruz, farther away than their people who had come from one of the islands in the Caribbean. Some of them were still being sold in the old days, as if they were cattle or horses."

Speaking to her daughter, the mother saw the breasts of her young daughter. She imagined them puckered like lips for a man's mouth. They were beginning to push out against the blouse. The miracle had begun and there was nothing the mother could do.

"Love is a curse," the mother told her daughter. "It casts a spell on people. It makes people dream. It makes others delirious. For some the longing to be merged with another is unbearable to the point of pain. Exquisite agony, some people say. There are few joys quite as marvelous and sweet as that of two beings mating, but love is bittersweet," the voice said. "At the very climax of joy there is always a yearning lamentation for what you are about to lose. That is why some people cry when they make love. Because along with an immensity of tenderness, loving also brings sorrow and pain. But be careful, *hijita.* Some men do not respect the woman who shares her love and passion. *¡Hombres jodidos! Unos no más quieren levantarle la falda a una mujer ... bajarle los calzones ... y pos, ¿pa que te digo? Vienen, se la meten a uno, se duermen y se van. ¡Amor! ... ¡mierda pa ese tipo de hombre!* Such men do not deserve a woman's passion, I tell you. But what is there to do?"

The voice continued. Speaking in Spanish, the mother told her what all the family wanted to keep secret. *Debes saber, hija, que una de tus bisabuelas era mulata.* "One of your great-grandmothers, she had blue eyes and blond hair, like you. Yes, the blood ... *la sangre de negros y árabes y judíos corre por tu sangre* ... yes, the blood of Africans and Jews and Arabs runs through your veins, even though you have blue eyes and blond hair. You must know, *hija,* that one day you may give birth to a dark-skinned baby. Some of our people have turned their backs on their own children if they look like our ancestors. Our obstinate blood comes back. Sometimes it skips a generation. Sometimes it comes back in one member of a family only. No matter who becomes your husband," she added. And when the daughter asked from which side of the family the mulata came, her mother answered that it did not matter. "Anyway, the mulata was sold, and years later after bearing many children who are your ancestors, she was freed. She lived a long life. She was nearly a hundred years old when she died. Good genes come from her in our family. But, I was saying, love is a curse."

The woman's voice was the voice of destiny, the voice of ancestral blood, speaking in his dream. Even in his sleep Miguel was conscious of wanting to understand women. But the voice was not making sense at all. Now the voice began to chant, to sing. The voice was singing songs of love, blood, death, and of passions aflame. The voice was singing that love is the flame that consumes lovers, the wind that one inhales, the sea on which one drifts.

More songs followed. They conjured up in the dreamer's mind images of young, sensuous women dancing, whose small breasts were strong and firm. They were women who were cursed or blessed with a hunger for love like men. The songs conjured up images of long flowing skirts that swirled about and revealed beautiful well-shaped legs that seemed to open from time to time, inviting love like a fertile garden longs for seeds. And in the dream the women's long flowing skirts pressed and flowed like running water between their legs and against the secret parts where love dwelled.

Breathtaking images of young women without men, dancing a sensuous ballet together. Veritable spectacle of breasts with hardened nipples, legs open and inviting, glimpses of sexual ecstasy, mouth and lips partly open, inhaling and exhaling heavily, loudly, passions aflame. Dancing. Young women's bodies caught up in a torrent of passion. A dream-ballet of passion. Young women filled with desire that awakens corresponding desire in men, against men's will, in accordance with nature's laws. During all the ages of life, there have been young women who wish not to be barren, who long for love, as men do … .

Tu sangre … Your blood, the voice continued, this time speaking to the dreamer, comes from all the continents of the world. Your blood has the power of rivers and oceans and storms. Your blood is poisoned by jealousy, by too large hearts that accommodate many loves. The poisoned blood flows from one generation to another. One never knows when the blood will flare up again. Vengeful ghosts will appear. Winds and storms and waves will make the flames of desire leap again. Nakedness is strange and wonderful. The voice of the sea speaks seductively, its hissing whispers, the lapping waves murmur, clamor like the waves of passion within; the sea invites the soul to wander and to drift and to dream about forbidden love.

Love is an exquisite curse. If love makes you weep, you will know that you have been cursed with the flaming passion of the ancestor, she who later found her way into a history book, where a small entry recorded the date on which she was sold by a widow. She is only a whisper in our family ... *la mulata blanca* is a secret. From one generation to another, her blood appears again in her progeny.

You, dreamer with your dark skin, are one of her progeny, the voice said. Perhaps you will know love. It may be that full skirts and strong legs, breasts and secret parts of women will make you weep. The blood comes aflame. Winds and rains, storms and hurricanes bring out the wild, untamed blood. It is passed on, from generation to generation. You have inherited lust and passion. Some will see it as a weakness or a curse. Others will see passion as a strength. Some will laugh. But for many years you will not be able to laugh about it because it will rule your life. If you think of it as a gift, perhaps the power of your mind can make it so.

Toward the end of the dream that made little sense to him, before Miguel awakened, he became keenly aware that he was dreaming, dreaming that he was begging to be cursed with love. Curse me! Let the blood of my white mulata ancestor leap into flames again. Let the drums enflame the blood. Drums, *cumbanchas*, sticks, wooden instruments, emit your deep, hard-wooded, musical and sensual sounds, awaken the body's desire for voluptuous pleasures. Bring back the love that lives on in the scent of jasmine and wild tropical flowers, that lingers on in the lush smell and frothy sounds of the Caribbean Sea; bring back the body's rhythms that connect us with the forces of nature and with the powerful movements of sea tides and waves. Let my blood sing and dance. Let the voice of the blood, the voice of my destiny, the voice of the wind that I inhale, the voice of the sea on which I was born to drift—let the voice speak and make me delirious, joyfully delirious, even though in pain. At the very climax of joy let me cry out with despair, with a yearning lamentation for an irretrievable loss.

Miguel awakened with desire and longing for voluptuous pleasures. His plea had been heard. Even though he could not understand what the dream meant, he cherished the intensity of his passionate longings. He remembered an entry in his notebook that he made while he was watching Carlos Saura's film, *Amor brujo*, about bewitching gypsy love, and about love that persists after death. The film had reminded him of a play that he saw a few years ago, García Lorca's *Yerma*. He wrote:

> Las mujeres *de García Lorca, like those of Tennessee Williams, are women wounded by love. Women in* Amor brujo *and* Yerma. *A swirl of big, wide skirts that celebrate the bodies they cover but also reveal; a ballet of proud breasts that point upward, haughtily; one woman longing for a man, her husband, to spill his seeds in her; gypsy passion transformed into art.*

What puzzled him the most about the dream was the part about the mulata, the white woman of African ancestry with blond hair and blue eyes. Slowly however, he began to connect his dream with the film, with a book about a woman who swims out into the water at the end, and with the trip to the village of his father's birth, seven months before his father's ninetieth birthday.

During that visit, while looking through documents at the Cerralvo Bureau of Vital Statistics (el Registro Civil de Cerralvo, Nuevo

León) he had come across an entry in one of the long gray ledgers that listed business transactions, the buying and selling of lands, houses, cattle, chickens, goats, horses, and other possessions. On page 28 of the Archivo Municipal ledger, he came across a fascinating entry by accident, written in the most beautifully elegant handwriting, dated and labeled, 1718, XII, folio 181, no. 77: *Doña María García Guerra, mujer legítima de don Antonio Fernández Vallejo, vecina de esta ciudad, vende a don Diego José de Barreda, vecino de la villa de Monterrey, una mulata blanca, esclava, sujeta a servidumbre, llamada María de edad de veintidós años, poco más o menos.* There was more.

In his mind that day the brief entry became a treatise on Mexican colonial society, slavery as a legal and economic institution, illiteracy, miscegenation and ancestry. During the preceding seven or eight years dark-skinned people had come increasingly into Miguel's dreams, especially women, for whom his fascination had grown over the years, inexplicably, as if his blood were searching its remotest origins in other continents of the world.

Doña María García Guerra, according to the Municipal Archives document, a resident of the city, was sold to don Diego José de Barreda, resident of the city of Monterrey, a white mulata of twenty-two years of age, also named María, legally owned by the seller, once the legal wife and now the widow and legal beneficiary of don Antonio Fernández Vallejo, from whom she had inherited the light-skinned young woman of African and Visigothic ancestry. As was common among slaves, her age was approximate. The exact date of slaves' or their children's births were hardly ever known on account of there being no written records of when they were born, and also because children of slaves were often taken away from their mothers shortly after they were born, and sold.

Like other slaves the young white mulata did not know her mother or her father. The entry in the Municipal Archives document also stated that the young woman was being sold free of encumbrances, shared ownerships, and indebtedness, and free of illness, madness, and such defects as thievery. She was sold for 300 pesos in gold *reales*, in accordance with legal procedure, at the office of the *alcalde ordinario* of that city, duly witnessed by men whose names appear on the record: Francisco Sánchez de Robles, Francisco de Larralde, and Domingo Miguel Guajardo, the latter of whom signed for the seller, who stated that she could not. The document was dated at Villa de Cerralvo, Nuevo León, 31 December 1718.

There was no mention of the light that came into the eyes of the buyer, but we can imagine the rest. A man in his fifties, don Diego José de Barreda now looked forward to the end of his celibacy. There was also no mention of the envious, lascivious look and the admiring glances in the eyes of the two witnesses when they contemplated the young slave woman with desire, with curled lips opening and closing, revealing restless tongues and a salivating mouth. There was no mention either of the slave woman's two little girls, beautiful like the mother, one darker than the other, both sired by the deceased don Antonio, whose ages were five and seven, who would remain in the possession of doña María. The little girls would grow up and they would bring children into the world, and as slaves they would increase doña María's wealth. More than a hundred years would pass before Mexico would become independent of Spain. Eventually slavery would be made illegal.

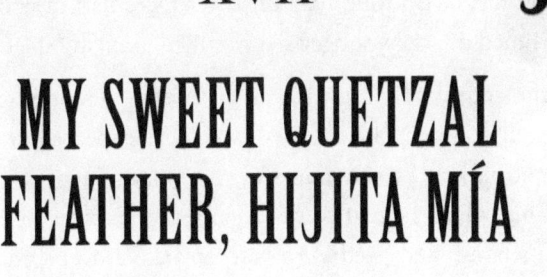

XVII

MY SWEET QUETZAL FEATHER, HIJITA MÍA

In axcan noconetzin, cocotzin, nocihuapiltzin ... auh in tehuatl ma timoxiccauh, ma timonecauh, in tinocozqui, in tinquetzal; ma ontlami immitzin ... .

Ahora mi niñita, tortolita, mujercita ... y, tú, no te abandones, no seas desperdiciada, no te quedes atrás, tú que eres mi collar, mi pluma de quetzal; no se dañe tu rostro, tu corazón ... .

Libro de los Huehuehtlahtolli
(*Book of Wise Admonishments*)

On a path well known to the women of the village the older sister led the younger sister by the hand. The older sister was hastening the pace of the younger sister, tugging at her hand. Making their way through a wooded area, each sister in turn pushed aside the rough, prickly branches of shrubs and bushes. Sharp brambles cut into the skin of their arms. Little trickles of blood flowed from the cuts and scratches. There was no pain; they did not even notice the blood.

The younger sister was breathing with difficulty. She pulled back her older sister, who unwillingly allowed the girl a moment of rest before pulling her forward again. The older sister paused again for a few moments when they came upon the rubble of a temple where they had once worshipped Tloque Nahuaque.

The pale men with long hair on their faces had destroyed it. The two continued on, the younger sister pulled along by the older sister.

Now the sound of running water brought terror into the heart of the younger sister. She dreaded what was expected of her, by her mother and father, by the elders of the village. Her sister reminded her, told her what she had to do. Again, the younger sister pulled at her sister's hand. She needed to rest, to take a deep breath. She inhaled deeply, and feeling a contraction coming on, instinctively she blew the air from her lungs through her mouth, slowly. The older sister placed a comforting arm around the sister's shoulders and waited. Then they continued on.

Not yet fifteen years old, the younger sister was big with child. Her breasts and her ankles were swollen. The contractions were closer now, more frequent.

Finally they reached a place near the stream where it was not too deep, and the older sister halted. Here, the older sister pointed, and the younger sister squatted. Push. Push, the older sister ordered. A strong contraction came and the younger sister inhaled deeply and pushed. After what seemed a very long time she could feel the head of the child opening her up. She grunted and panted. The effort to expel the child was long and exhausting.

She dreaded what the child would look like. Pushing hard she thought of how she had become fascinated, almost from the moment they arrived, with the men who had long hair on their faces. She thought of the restlessness that they had awakened in her.

Hidden from their view she had watched the young naked men when they bathed in the streams. The sight of their naked bodies, of the profusion of hair on their faces and on their bare chests hardened her nipples, brought strange, mysterious sensations between her legs—where now she felt the pain of a child wanting to be born. One of the young strangers, more than the others, had appealed to her.

She had sensed a vulnerability about him, similar to her own. He had green eyes.

Her mother had spoken to her about womanhood. She had warned her about the strangers, had told her about the miracle of childbirth, about the importance of waiting. She must never bring shame to her mother and father, to the elders and to their people. Her mother had made clear to both daughters that their women had to use a very unpleasant method to undo the shame of consorting with the bearded strangers.

She had not heeded her mother's admonishments. Her body seemed to have been commanded by great forces of nature. During restless hours of the night, and during idle moments during the day, she was visited by mysterious, inexplicable longings that made her body swell and flow, and float like a piece of wood on water. When she could no longer bear the strange, passionate longings she went to the man with the golden hair on his face. He was young and inexperienced, but she discovered while their bodies were moving to the rhythms of ancient atavistic powers that she could will the anticipated pleasure and take it from his body. She had come to him when the honey was already flowing inside her body. Hastily and awkwardly the young man responded to her yielding. Despite his haste and awkwardness her pleasure had come from her own desire.

Now, squatting and pushing, in her consciousness she could hear her mother's words. At that moment the words and the strong contractions dispelled the images of the delirious short-lived pleasure. Her mother's words had been spoken with love and tenderness not long ago, when the change had come upon her body, when her mother told her that she had reached child-bearing age.

Push, push, her sister ordered. Inhaling deeply, then pushing hard, panting, the pregnant girl heard again her mother's words of endearment. *Hijita mía, mi palomita, mujercita.* She pushed and panted.

Hijita, fruit of my womb, her mother said, I gave birth to you, your father and I raised you, and to us you are a precious jewel, a fine stone that we polished together. True, this life brings much trouble and hardship that exhaust our energies. Yet we must exercise great diligence to attain our wishes and desires, and ask that the gods favor us with their blessings …. *Auh in tehaual ma timoxiccauh, ma timonencauh, ma timoteputz-cauh … hijita … precious jewel … my quetzal feather, let nothing lead you astray … let nothing harm your face and heart … oh, my child!* ….

She inhaled deeply, held her breath momentarily, grunted and pushed. She could feel the baby's head tearing at the flesh of her body, the same flesh that had taken pleasure for the first time with the inexperienced young, bearded man. It had been intense, feverish, mysterious, delirious pleasure. Now she might have to pay the price, the loss of her newborn, for not listening to her mother … . *¡Ay, hijita! mi pluma de quetzal* ….

From downstream, as in a bad dream, came the screaming of women giving birth. The screams, the grief and anguish of other women and girls were heart-rending. Her heart filled with remorse, she prayed. Oh, I pray that my baby will not be white. I pray to Tloque Nahuaque that his complexion will be dark like that of our people so that I will not have to drown him. The baby's head is completely out now, the older sister tells her. Push, push. My hands are reaching in now. I can feel the baby's shoulders. My hand has found an arm. I am moving my fingers under the baby's arm. My fingers are looking for the other arm. Push, push. I have him. His shoulders are out … push, push, oh, *mi hermanita*, my little sister … he is slipping out more easily now, the baby is completely out now. Oh, *hermanita*, the baby is so beautiful, *como una pluma de quetzal*. Just listen to her cry. Look, your baby is a girl. Her skin is neither white or dark. Her hair is dark, like ours, her eyes are green, but her skin … . Oh, what are we supposed to do? Shall she live or die? We are supposed to drown only the ones who are born white. What are we to do with this infant?

XVIII

WE DID NOT CHOOSE OUR FATHERS

Every year brings with it multitudes of this class of slaves ...
a very different-looking class of people are springing up at
the south, and are now held in slavery, from those originally
brought to this country from Africa ... [T]housands are
ushered into the world, annually, who, like myself owe their
existence to white fathers, and those fathers most frequently
their own masters.

Narrative of the Life of Frederick Douglass

What were we to do? What choices did we have? Fifty years after the fall of México-Tenochtitlán many of us had been born. We were restless and confused. Our fathers were the bearded men who rejected and abandoned our indigenous mothers. They came across the waters on great floating houses. When the floating houses reached our lands, the huge bearded stranger-monsters with four legs moved swiftly and attacked our warriors. Their hands had the power of fire and thunder. They enlisted the assistance of our own people, who were subjects of our great leaders. The bearded strangers and the subjects resented the power of our leaders. Our brave warriors fought against our own people. They were our subjects and they allied themselves with the strangers because they resented us. Our brave warriors fought against the bearded strangers despite the fear of their flame and thunder. Our brave warriors fell in battle, bleeding and in pain. Thousands upon thousands died. There were many battles between the bearded strangers and our people. Much blood was shed. I do not want to remember those days that the codices would tell us were filled with death and sorrow.

For many of us childhood was miserable. We lived among other children who were like ourselves, but different from children of our native people. We knew that the bearded strangers were our fathers. Our mothers were despised by some of our people for having children with the strangers, and we were despised too, especially if we looked like them.

Some mothers, on the other hand, were praised for introducing into the blood of our people the blood of the strangers who had waged war against our warriors and won. Also, some of our women were sexually attracted to *los negros*, and they wanted to have children with them because they too were *conquistadores*. They were powerful, very strong men. They spoke the language of the bearded strangers. Because some of our women found the dark men sexually attractive they entered into unions with the *negros* for the sexual pleasure alone. Children were born in this manner, of course. We did not choose our fathers.

The stench of blood and death lasts for a long time. Even after the stench went away it remained in my nostrils.

It was not easy to be mestizos—children of the strangers, *blancos o negros*. When our fathers rejected us, we were scorned by our half-brothers and by our cousins, and often by our mothers' people.

On our mothers' side we shared family and ancestors. On our fathers' side, we had ancestors too. Surely, across the great waters we had great-grandparents, grandparents, aunts and uncles from our fathers' side. But if our fathers abandoned us how could we ever know them. We were despised mestizos. As children we were not allowed near our half brothers and half sisters, the *blancos*.

Abandoned, we were nothing to our fathers' people. How then

could we be anything in the eyes of our mother's people? Some among us of mixed blood were fortunate. If we were born white and our fathers accepted us, whether our mothers were *indias* or *negras*, we were taught our fathers' language and their culture. We were brought up with their religion, in our fathers' homes. We were *españolados*, the children of *conquistadores*. We counted.

Some of us were unfortunate if our fathers rejected us, if we were born with skin that was white. For children born to *indias*, rejected by our fathers, it was better to be born dark. In our mothers' indigenous culture some of our people insisted that if native women gave birth against their will to white babies they must drown them. These women went to give birth by streams. Babies were easy to drown that way, just as soon as they were born. Who were we then?

We were not like our mothers or our fathers, a little of each, even when we were children of mothers and fathers who were *indios*, *negros*, and *estranjeros*. Years later, other children were born of our indigenous women and the bearded strangers, and in addition because the bearded strangers brought *los negros* to our communities other children had black fathers. Many years after I was born, when I was a grown man, I was told that I was born a white baby to a native woman. I did not know until I was a man that I was not a white *mulato*.

In childhood I never knew my mother or my father. *La negra* who raised me was my mother, whether she gave birth to me or not. I was not born of the *negra's* womb, I found out many years later, but she saved my life. There is a saying among our people that a mother is the woman who raises a child whether or not the child came from her womb. It makes sense.

La negra, the woman I called *Mamá*, told me that when my indigenous mother was going to drown me because of my white skin she took pity on me. Instead of drowning me my real mother abandoned me, left me to die by the creek. My mother took pity on me and could not drown me.

La negra found me. A newborn, I was crying for a mother's milk. I was soiled, she told me. *Ella era una esclava,* she was a slave. She was the woman who raised me and whom I learned to love as a mother. I found out about my origins many years later when I was a grown man. She told me.

She already had two sons, but there was enough love in her heart to love another child, even one who was white. In appearance at least, a *güero,* for I was a mestizo, a bastard, she told me. When I was grown, she told me that my mother was taken by force.

La negra brought me up to believe that I was a white mulato. How could I know? Many white *mulatos* were born years after the fall of Tenochtitlán after slavery began, and a large number of mestizos. Whatever I was, I was a mestizo. I was neither this nor that.

I was educated by missionaries. My teachers were Fray Bernardino de Sahagún, Mendietta, Motolinía. I learned fast, Latin, Greek, Spanish, and Náhuatl. I was a bastard who might have been drowned by his mother because my skin was white, different from hers. But look how the African woman brought me up. The men with beards also fathered other children with the slave women. Some of them had blue, others had green eyes. One of my mother's sons had green eyes like mine. Could his father, I always wondered, have been my father too? How could we know? Sometimes the priests did not record our births, or they would include statements in the birth certificates to identify us as mixed race bastard children sired by *conquistadores.* And they were always careful not to name the priests who were our fathers.

We did not choose our fathers, I always say. Growing up as we did, scorned by people of our mothers' villages and by our fathers' people, the strangers to our lands, what could people expect of us?

I finally joined a group of discontented people like myself. Vagabundos, they called us—wanderers and misfits—they were angrier than I would ever be. We grew up to be men, and we used to raid villages, plunder, and kill.

Discontented men, we stole women and brought them back to our communities. Men without women are no good. We were despised men. Decent men would not have us marry their decent daughters and have us as sons-in-law. So we took women from all communities; they were white, mulatas, mestizas, and newly-arrived African slaves. We picked and took the women that we preferred.

Some of these women would not resign themselves to their fates. They did not respond to the men's attentions. These women were always morose and difficult. Other women resigned themselves, reluctantly. They had no choice. A few women captivated younger men. Slowly, affection was born and they began to love one another, and they raised families. Eventually their families forgot that the women had been stolen. The women lost contact with their families. They formed families of their own, and hundreds of years later some even wanted to trace their genealogies back, far back, even beyond their generation, far back across the great waters.

Some missionaries would also write about us for posterity. We needed and wanted women, some wrote. One understanding woman writer would say of us later that we were young men with steel rods between our legs.

We were no different than our progenitors, the men who came on the floating houses that arrived upon the shores of our lands. A wise man expressed sympathy about them. Quite simply they were men, he said, who had been without women for months. Their desire for the native women and later for *las negras*—our mothers—was natural, to be expected. But, some of us could not contain the rage against our fathers that began with rejection in childhood.

When we were little boys, some of us knew that one day we would get revenge on the fathers that we did not choose. In my case, one day I met my father and I killed him. I do not want to remember the violence and rage in my heart. After I killed him, gazing at his corpse I looked into his face. To this day I see his face every morning when I look at my reflection in a stream. In my young years I did not know my father or what he looked like. Now, the father I did not choose is dead. No one chooses their mother and father.

XIX

MY FATHER'S FRIEND ALEX

Several times my brother, Antonio Jr., had spoken of a very close friend of our father, who would be able to tell many stories about him. The man, who knew our father well, felt, however, that he did not know me well enough to be open, so I decided to write to him. I wanted to put him at ease, to let him know that my father had shared some of his secrets, subtly and indirectly, as well as directly.

I wrote and told the man whose name is Alex Velásquez that over a period of several years I had collected my father's stories about his entire life. Of course, I made clear, he was discreet about matters of the heart, about women in his life—*era muy discreto mi padre, muy respetuoso.*

Nevertheless, I knew that my father was a man who loved women. I wrote that his eyes and his hands, like my own, had a life of their own. They are difficult to control. In my childhood memories I remember his driving our Model A Ford to Pflugerville, and it was evident even to my mother that his eyes would be irresistibly drawn to women that he saw walking along our route. His eyes took in the rhythms of their pace, the movements of buttocks and legs and breasts. He never stopped looking. *¡Sinvergüenza!* my mother used to say. *Pay attention to your driving.*

It was my mother's objections to my father's admiring glances of women that called my child's attention to what he was doing. I too am compelled to look and to admire the beauty of women.

One day I asked: *Papá, ¿cuando deja un hombre de sentir pasión por las mujeres?* He was eighty-five or eighty-six at the time. He glanced upwardly and into his mind. Reflecting but a moment, he responded.

—*No sé, hijo. Quiensabe. Creo que nunca.*

He was that way until he died, I believe, judging by the last time that I saw him, three weeks before he died. I have shared with other people my experience of having visited with him in the nursing home where he spent the last month of his life. Unfortunately, his hearing no longer permitted him what may have been among the greatest joys of his life, the company and the conversation of other storytellers like himself, men and women with extraordinary memories of their long lives. What a heart-warming experience it was to see him courting the elderly ladies there. To eavesdrop, unintentionally, on his eloquent expressions of a widower's unfulfilled longings, his lamenting that it is not natural for man or woman to be alone, regardless of age. His language was beautiful and poetic when it came to expressing feelings of the heart.

It was otherwise when he became angry, and then it was his father's curses that he spouted forth. The cursing came in old age, and became second nature to my father. His eloquence came from three years of education at a Mexican village school, from memorizing the poetry of the three great Mexican poets of his childhood—Juan de Dios Peza, Manuel Acuña, and Antonio Plaza.

A few years after I became a university professor of literature, he asked me if I had heard of these poets. No, I said. *Otra vez es usted mi maestro,* I said. He loved knowing that he was a university professor's first great teacher, and he was immensely proud each time that I thanked him for having begun to teach me, when I was eight years old and learning English, how to read and write Spanish. In childhood, he truly was *mi primer gran maestro,* and he prepared me for the other *gran maestro,* the university professor who directed the entire direction of my life.

My father had a fine village school teacher who taught traditional disciplines excellently, who instilled in the boy a love of learning that was systematic and well organized. My father always spoke of the Spanish language that he learned as *el castellano*, the Castilian language. He loved poetry and patriotic verses, which he learned to recite from memory. Well into his seventies and eighties he could recite poetry that he had learned by heart when he was seven or eight years old. He could still do so on the occasion of his ninetieth birthday, when my brother and I took him back to Cerralvo, Nuevo León, where he was born. Three weeks before he died I asked him to recite a patriotic poem about Mexican Independence, and he did.

In the course of his life many people had to have heard his stories. Some younger men with whom he worked, he used to tell me, disbelieved some of the remarkable stories that he told about his life. They were astonished to hear him recite poetry that he had learned as a boy. They called him a liar. To my father, his long life was a source of awe and wonder.

At the nursing home my father was always bathed, shaven, and clean. He would sit up straight in his wheel chair. Wearing his false teeth that made him look twenty or twenty-five years younger he attracted the attention of one lovely, small, blue-eyed woman, Mildred Smith, a Texan of Irish background. One day I noticed her gazing at my father with admiring eyes. Then she looked to me and told me that my father was a handsome man. He certainly was. My father did not hear her say so.

My father told me many stories about himself that Alex very likely may have heard. I mentioned them in my letter. One stands out in my mind. In the family it came to be known as the *macho blanco* story. My father told it in front of my mother to several of us in the family.

A few months before he and my mother got married they had to have a physical examination. Laughter interrupted his story-telling when he was describing his examination in the doctor's office.

—A nurse, he said, breaking into a hearty laugh, accidentally touched my member, and in the blink of an eye there it was, rearing up like the *macho blanco* that my father owned, ready to mate twenty-four hours a day it seemed. The nurse looked and saw the size of it. *Oh, oh!* the nurse said. Her eyes were wide open with shock, ha ha, and she dashed out of the examining room. Then the doctor rushed in to see what was wrong. Seeing what had frightened his nurse, the doctor said, *oh yeah, oh yeah, this boy he ready for to get married.*

Those were my father's words, which he repeated in his accented English after another round of raucous laughter. *Oh yeah! This boy, he ready for to get married.* Another story that he loved to tell to make people laugh was about a young man, who knew that my father was the father of twins. Again, in my father's own language, he said, *el muchacho me preguntó how you makee twins, señor? How you makee twins?* And my father told him, *fuckee, fuckee, fuckee. Alla time fuckee.* My father was hilarious with laughter. My mother was playfully shocked. She understood what he was saying. We will never know how much English she knew.

My father was born with the gift of laughter. His physical energy was also exceptional. Nature does not distribute sexual energy equally. Some receive much more than others, and in those of warm and gentle hearts, a large energy is the source of playfulness about it, because it is a gift that leads people in and out of embarrassing situations.

About his young manhood, when he was in his forties, he told me stories. He worked for the Hot Shot Delivery and the Two-Nickel Delivery during the war years. The drivers for the two services were supposed to deliver groceries and other kinds of purchases, but they were clandestine taxi drivers who transported people. Being discreet, my father did not talk about women that he met or knew. He told me about men who went into the cantinas on Sixth Street, for us, *la calle seis,* and about some of the passengers who pulled knives or guns on him, and about men who were either drunk or had taken drugs. He remembered those days fifty years later, when I drove him from Premont, Texas, to and from Austin. He was ninety-three years old.

The intimacy of the automobile journey was relaxing to both of us and put him in a reminiscing, storytelling frame of mind. He told me countless stories about the war years in the 1940s, some of which he had told me before. By then I was like a father looking after a child. Story after story spilled from his heart and memory.

—One of your mother's aunts, he said, was a troublemaker. She told your mother that she saw me with women on Sixth Street. It made your mother always suspect that I was out with women all the time when I was out working, when we were very poor. During the war years, coming home from the Two-Nickel at two or three in the morning I used to sleep only about three hours. Then I would get up at five in the morning to go my daytime job in construction. I never needed much sleep.

Another memory came to mind that I did not mention in my letter. Never once in my entire adult life did my father ever mention how I once created difficulties between him and my mother. I was nine or ten years old. One day I was going through my father's coat pockets, looking for coins as I usually did. I found a nickel and a little tin aspirin container in one of the pockets. I tucked the nickel into my pocket and returned the little container to the pocket. A few minutes later my mother complained of a terrible headache. And there are no aspirins in the house, she said. On hearing this I told her that my father had a box of aspirins in his coat pocket. She went for his coat that I had placed on the back of the chair in another room. In a moment I heard my mother's angry voice.

—¡Sinvergüenza! What are these things doing in your pocket?

My father said that a friend had asked him to keep them for him. ¡Mentiroso! She struck him with her fists. He raised his powerful arms and took her wrists firmly in his hands so that she would not hurt herself.

Get out of this house! *¡Sálte de esta casa, sinvergüenza!*

My mother's intense anger towards my father was incomprehensible to me. My father never lifted a hand to my mother, in their entire life. For reasons inexplicable to me at that age, my mother stayed angry a long time and made my father sleep in his truck for several nights.

A few years later I made a purchase at a drugstore. Once back in the car, looking forward to my date that night, I took my purchase out of the little paper sack and looked at the picture of an elegant peacock on the lid of the little tin container. I understood at that moment what I had done. In my young manhood, this memory of having unknowingly betrayed my father returned again and again to bother me.

As a man I wanted very much to understand my father on a man-to-man basis. I thought back to the years after my youngest brother was born, I wrote, when my father worked nights for the Two-Nickel Delivery. I remembered hearing my parents' whispered voices in the early morning hours. By then I was twelve. Their bedroom was right next to the room in which my brothers and I slept. On some nights, through the wall I could hear my mother, always annoyed, telling my father to move away to his side of the bed. *Don't touch me,* her voice said. *We have too many children already. We can barely buy food for the ones we have.* On other nights I would hear my mother's voice, annoyed as usual. *Aha, aha! Look at yourself, going to sleep so peacefully. Content. Staying on your side of the bed, ¿eh? ¿Dónde has estado?*

As a man I reflected and understood. My father was forty-three years old when my youngest brother was born. No more children after this one, my mother told my father peremptorily. Inadvertently, she told me when she was telling me about the birth of my youngest brother. To my mother, understandably concerned about the large family that we already were, having no more children meant total abstinence. What was my father to do? During his forties when his physical energy was healthy my father understandably needed what my mother denied him. If he touched her at night my mother became annoyed. If he did not, she was annoyed. My mother's feelings went farther. She resented him for having the most natural manly desires, and for the rest of her life my mother harbored resentment towards my father.

About those memories of the little tin box, I did not write in my letter to Alex. In my letter I wrote that well into his eighties, my father still had eyes for the ladies. After he died I received letters from some of the women for whom he worked as a gardener. They told me so. I am moved by these women's candor and especially by their compassion and understanding. What beautiful souls they are to be amused by the natural propensities of an old man, with which Nature endows some human beings and by the embarrassing situations they create. Apparently, *el macho blanco* never went to sleep, contrary to my father's saying playfully that it had.

Another story that my father told me comes to mind. A friend of his, also in his eighties, was in the hospital, dying. He had but a few days to live, according to the medical prognosis. He was alert, however, and whenever the nurses came to attend to him, my father said, the man could not help himself. His hands would come alive with longing, and he would touch the nurses. This octogenarian begged his grown son, my father told me, to bring him a woman so that he could die happily. The son refused. The man begged. Again and again the father begged and the son refused. Finally, the son's heart was moved, and he brought a woman for his father. A little after that the man died happily. Now is this not a fitting conclusion to my letter? I think it was that story that made me ask my father: when does a man lose his desire for women?

My letter ends with a request for memories about my father, of every kind. I said that I would be especially grateful to know some stories about his years with the Two-Nickel Service Delivery. When I put the letter in an envelope I telephoned my brother Antonio to let him know it would go out in the next day's mail, and to call or visit Alex in a few days. In a few days I will be in Austin and my brother will take me to see him in person.

XX

COLLECTOR OF STORIES

Nadie pudo
Recordarlas después: el viento
Las olvidó, el idioma del agua
Fue enterrado, las claves se perdieron
O se inundaron de silencio o sangre.

...

Yo estoy aquí para contar la historia.

No one could
remember them afterward: the wind
forgot them, the language of water
was buried, the keys were lost
or flooded with silence or blood.

...

I am here to tell the story.

Pablo Neruda, "A Lamp on Earth," *Canto General*

Notebook entry, August 22. *Since the first time when I visited the Confederate Cemetery in Austin, Texas, strolling through cemeteries has always inspired me to write. I was about twelve years old at the time. Now that I am no longer young the separate cemetery for Mexicans in Pflugerville, Texas, makes me think about history and the past. Whenever I visit this town that was settled by*

German people I remember the children of different backgrounds with whom I went to school. Since I was a child the faces of children whose parents or grandparents came from different parts of the world fascinated me. We Mexican children went to school with children whose ancestors had come from England, Czechoslovakia, Germany, Poland, Ireland, Lebanon, and other places.

Intuitively, somehow my child's perceptions enabled me to recognize in the faces of childhood classmates their different ancestries as we were growing up. Sitting with them in the same classrooms we learned to read and write English. We learned to diagram sentences. In the old days we had spelling and penmanship classes. Our teachers were magnificently old-fashioned and they were all English grammarians. Most were un-married. We were their children. For them, teaching was a calling. I cherish them to this day.

On one of my visits to Austin I drove by the building that used to be Palm Elementary School. The building brought back fond memories of superb teachers who taught us English, arithmetic, spelling and penman-ship, science, and social studies.

As a writer of fiction I am immensely fascinated by ancestry. I marvel at the magic of heredity. Only after traveling and living in many parts of the world did I discern how richly varied also were the faces of Mexi-can people with whom I grew up. Many like myself had norteño ances-tors. We knew we were Mexican, and we used to speak of the others with blue eyes and blond hair as americanos.

In those days of segregated schools the law did not allow colored peo-ple, as African Americans were called, to go to school with us. To mexi-canos they were negros (in Spanish), and to white people they were Negroes or colored, and niggers to others. I do not know when I first heard the words white people, but to this day the words white people cause me discomfort, and now, forty years after a university teaching career, I understand why.

My experience and perceptions did not confirm what scholars and the average person say about race. After many years of studying race and ethnicity I, a born iconoclast, refute scholarly notions, misconceptions and erroneous perceptions of race. These falsehoods, I have learned, have been imposed on our minds by educated racethinkers, scientists and social scientists, educators and scholars through their lectures, scholarly papers, and books. History and experience tell me that no matter who formulates and expresses them, and regardless of their credentials, scholarly- and pseudo-scientifically based race perceptions are unreliable, misleading, and frequently false.

Since childhood, my classmates, as well as books and learning to read, developed in me a preponderant interest in all peoples, cultures, nations, and languages. This interest of the child became a major characteristic of the person that I am today. They were, after all, not much different from Mexicans in appearance, except for those of us who were darker.

When I try to explain this interest, this fascination—born of personal contact with human beings, and through books, language, and travel— I conclude that it is due first of all to the accident of birth, of being a Mexican born in the United States. My elementary school teachers told me that because of my birth I was an American. I believed them. Secondly, I was born and destined—inexplicably—to develop this fascination with people of other lands.

My interest began to take systematic intellectual shape later. In my young manhood, I was a post graduate scholarship student at the National Autonomous University of Mexico (UNAM). From reading books that my professors recommended, I learned that by the sixteenth century the land of my ancestors had been a place of convergence of peoples of diverse ancestries. That opened my eyes to the ancient Mediterranean world.

Still later, the interest in the history of the country of my birth developed out of necessity and curiosity. As a writer, I look back on forma-

tive experiences quickened by emotional and intellectual curiosity. After coming to Ríoseco University in 1972 I wanted desperately to understand the anger and hostility that was attending social changes after 1954. Slowly, I began to understand.

In the 1970s the United States and California were becoming places where peoples of many nations, cultures, and languages were converging. With an enlarged understanding of the present I began to better understand the past. My interest in historiography grew. My writer's curiosity and my passion for learning knew no limits. There was about my reading a voracious quality that the greatest professor I have ever known easily discerned many years ago in my first graduate seminar paper.

From time to time I take his three-page typed critique of that scholarly paper and read it. I cherish that critique. My indebtedness to Ron Artmann grows each time I read the thoughtful words that he wrote. Many years later his novels and poetry would help me to understand why we had so much in common.

My romantic nature leads me to believe that my great interest in other peoples is due, however, to the convergence in my person and in our people at large of genes and chromosomes that represent many ancestries of the world. Our ancestries are multiple and millenary. Consequently, I have inherited from my ancestors—in genes and chromosomes—a variety of propensities that are to be found in all parts of the world.

Even though I was born far inland, beneath immense skies and among immense distances, I am like some of my ancestors, who having been born by the sea knew the attraction of unknown horizons. I, too, was destined to wander, to know many loves, to visit and know many cities and places. Some of us who wander are blessed or condemned never to return to the places where we were born. Far from our ancestors' tribes and clans and peoples, and far from our families and the places that they once inhabited, our ancestors' blood lives on in genes and chromosomes. I cherish the memories of the elders.

As a writer, I am of that race of people who, inspired by grief and sorrow, are born to turn sorrow into song, into art. As artists, we are born to be witnesses and to remember, to snatch from the wind the spoken stories that were never set down in writing, to rescue from oblivion the stories that history has silenced.

My sister and my brothers laugh when I tell them playfully that heredity singled me out for the family madness that should have been distributed among us. They are amused when I say, more accurately perhaps, that what accounts for the intensity of my propensities, appetites, and obsessions is that the madness of countless generations of our ancestors has converged on me. As I reach the end of the notebook in which I have been writing pages of my autobiography, and from a bird's eye view of Mexican history, I contemplate the ancient places where the great, so-called races of the world came together in the Central Valley of Mexico.

I close my eyes and hear the words of Pablo Neruda: Yo estoy aquí para contar la historia, *he wrote,* te busqué, padre mío / joven guerrero de tiniebla y cobre, o tú, planta nupcial, cabellera indomable,/ madre caimán, metálica paloma. *Eyes closed, I travel back hundreds of years, back to the republic of dreams. Later my ubiquitous spirit will wander from tent to tent among the* vagabundos, *the misfits and nonconformist vagabonds of* La Nueva España, *New Spain. I will listen to their words and hear their thoughts as well. From them, too, we Mexicans are descended:*

For thousands of years men who were seafarers, warriors, tradesmen, and conquerors traversed the lands around the Mediterranean Sea in all directions. Among the wanderers were statesmen, historians, philosophers, writers, and artists. It is reasonable to infer that since the beginning of time strangers, men and women, have been attracted to each other. Equally natural, when men have journeyed without women of their clans and tribes they found women in the many places to which they traveled. Consequently, the history of the world is a history of meetings and mating between men and women whose peoples have been from different geographical and cultural backgrounds, peoples who have worshipped different gods.

History books tell us that conquerors took women of the conquered by force. In seaports, cities, and villages, men who traveled and conquered also left women with child, with the strangers' genes and chromosomes fusing in the magic of creation.

It may be that some men were fated inevitably never to return to their native lands, and that by choice in countless cases men stayed willingly with women who opened their hearts and yielded their bodies to the strangers from afar. This is true of Gonzalo Guerrero, a Spaniard who was shipwrecked in 1511 off the coast of Yucatán, who married an indigenous princess, and sired the first mestizos in Mexico. In Mexico, he is known as the father of *mestizaje*. Three times after becoming a *cacique* among his adopted people he refused to be rescued by his countrymen, and he died in 1536 fighting as a leader of his adopted people against his countrymen.

Certain traits in human nature do not rule out men of gentle and kindly disposition to women. Such men counted among the conquerors. Surely such men must have loved the children born of indigenous women long ago, millennia before wars between tribes and clans over geographical boundaries and different gods stigmatized their unions and their progeny.

Today, thousands of years later, people who travel and those who reside in places where cultures have converged or begin to converge can trace for themselves the travels of genes and chromosomes. The travels are written in the physiognomies of people from different lands, in the shape of nose or eyelids, the color and texture of hair, in the color of the eyes and in the complexion.

No national, cultural, religious or language boundaries can conceal common ancestries of great antiquity, or the genes and chromosomes of ancestors who were brought together irrevocably by destiny. People can change their nationalities, culture, religions, and language; but they cannot change their ancestries.

Consider this. When seafaring men lost the fear of their ships' dropping away into the void at the horizon's edge the world changed. Men lost their fear after a bold madman with a dream embarked on a westward journey across the great unexplored ocean to find a passage to the East. Five hundred years later some descendants of Iberian people say that the courageous man stumbled and lost his way. In books, some men and women, presumably of learning and culture, wage a war of words among themselves; they intimidate each other into not praising certain historical events that they consider unworthy of being celebrated or commemorated, whether they be worthy or not.

Many others feel compelled to deny even the ancestries that they see in their faces in the mirror. The censorship, the intimidation and the denial of ancestry—these need to be understood. *Conquest, rape, colonization, domination, racism, genocide*—people use these words to deny their ancestors. These words are hurled against some of our ancestors, whose language some of us speak with respectful pride, ancestors whose customs and traditions give sense and meaning to our lives.

The arts must reconnect us with our ancestors and with our progeny. In the vast landscape of history, are inhumanities not to be found in some warring men of all times and places, to this very day? As a writer I believe it is well to remember that history is immutable. One should be watchful of people who are afflicted with historical amnesia. They follow a trend to judge the past simplistically, with ignorance, and others who know the past are intimidated into saying that two and two makes three.

My journey across history continues. Long before the madman set sail across the Atlantic and before the encounter between the people of three worlds, the codices of our indigenous ancestors tell us of a barbaric wandering people who came from a northern mythical land (called Aztlán many centuries later, and celebrated). They were people of a warrior nation who came and conquered a nation of peace-loving, cultured people whose countenances were made wise by flower and song and philosophy. The conquerors were wise, or perhaps clever, so they burned the codices—the history books of the peace-loving people—in order to erase their great wisdom and cultural achievements. Then the barbaric warriors, the *mexicas*, re-wrote the history books to aggrandize themselves, and to claim as their own the magnificent artistic achievements of the conquered people, *los toltecas*, which means artists, and they banished the conquered peoples' exemplary humanist, Quetzalcóatl. So say the codices.

To further aggrandize themselves the *mexicas*, ancestors of the *aztecas* took wives from among the cultured women of the conquered. Remaining warriors they adopted the culture of the conquered, and within a hundred years and more these warrior people found a place identified by an eagle with a serpent in its mouth atop a cactus, and there they established the capital of their empire. From *México-Tenochtitlán* as they named the city that they founded, they conquered and enslaved neighboring peoples of the central plateau. A time came when inexplicable events began to occur. Omens announced the coming of white-skinned bearded strangers. Were these events, the *aztecas* wondered, announcing the return of Quetzalcóatl? The time of the encounter came. This is what the codices say.

According to the codices the bearded strangers arrived in houses that floated on water. The Aztec warriors who took pride in a history of conquering and subjugating other people engaged the bearded strangers in battle. The bearded strangers were enormous beasts with four legs and they were part human. The *aztecas* thought that horse and man was one creature. Also, these mysterious beings could kill with flame and thunder. And between the two peoples the story of all human encounters, all conquests and domination, was played out again, in the human hearts of men and women brought together by destiny, and in the hearts of their progeny.

As they have since time began women played a most significant role. Five hundred years later the descendants of the women, whose people the great Explorer mistakenly called *Indian*, would still find their ancestry controversial. The women of what once used to be called the New World and men from the Mediterranean who were already mestizos created a new race, the history books later tell us, people in whom ancient amalgamations and millenary configurations of genes and chromosomes returned once more, miraculously. To this pool of genes and chromosomes Africa also contributed.

As a writer, I have been learning that the arts are especially suited to express the powerful drama of history that lives on in the hearts and spirits of descendants of people from Europe, from Asia, and from Africa. The visit to the Mexican cemetery in Pflugerville inspires me to revisit hushed and untold stories about our ancestors. Again, I close my eyes and in spirit I journey forward into the long ago past, across centuries, to wander from tent to tent through temporary en-campments. In imagination my writer's spirit drifts among ancestors, as I have wandered among the graves of my family in the separate Pflugerville cemetery for Mexicans. I listen to our ancestors' thoughts and eavesdrop on conversations that history has silenced and kept se-cret, in order to recover those hushed and untold stories. Listen:

More than five hundred years ago the sound of running water from nearby streams used to make the village girls of indige-nous ancestry tremble with fear. One day, in a small village like many others, a girl like countless other girls who preceded her, felt a terror in her heart. She listened to the water as she walked reluctantly toward the nearby stream, heartbroken about the task ahead. Her belly was full with a child that was ready to be born. Helped along by an older woman the girl walked awkwardly on swollen bare feet. The two women were making their way through thick bushes down toward the stream. They were following the path made by other girls and women to give birth to babies conceived against their will. The ritual of going to the streams began when the bearded men came and began to take girls and women by force.

Inside her body the seed of her womb wanted to burst free. *Remember*, the women of the village had told her, *if the child has light skin, you must drown it. You cannot keep a white child that looks like the man who violated you.* She stumbled and the older woman helped her, preventing her from falling. They were almost there. The crying of an infant ceased, and they knew that another mother had drowned her child. That is what she would have to do too, if the child was white. She wondered what her child would look like, and whether she would be able to keep her. Somehow, she sensed it would be a girl.

One of the black male slaves appeared at the Iberian man's tent to summon him. The woman from Africa has given birth, the black man said. It took a few minutes to finish some tasks at hand. Then he walked in the direction of the slave quarters. The labor had been long. He had told the slave not to bother him until the baby was born. Now he stood next to the cot on which the woman was resting, nursing the newborn infant, her child and his. Without speaking the woman looked up at the man. He wondered. What am I to do? How rosy the infant's complexion looked next to the African mother. She was one of the man's slaves.

He shifted the weight of his body and positioned himself in such a manner that he could easily make out the features of the newborn child. The nose and the nostrils were small and delicately shaped. The eyebrows were fine and so light in color that they were hardly visible. The infant's hair, still wet from the mother's amniotic fluid, was silky, only slightly darker. The father saw a streak of copper following the hairline around the front of the face. The baby's lips around the woman's nipple were small. He could tell, even though they were puckered. This child will definitely pass for Spanish, the man thought. There was no way for the man to know that the child, in growing up, would come to bear a remarkable resemblance to his own mother.

He wanted to know the sex of the newborn infant. When the man examined the infant, the mother anticipated his response. A child born to a slave is born a slave unless the father ... but no, it was foolish to have such thoughts. She would never be allowed to keep the infant. The man cursed loudly. He was disappointed because the newborn infant was a girl. He knew, and the mother knew, the fate of slave women's daughters, especially of those born with European features and light skin.

I could take her and raise her as Spanish, he thought, but what will happen when she becomes a woman, when she gets married and brings children into the world? Gazing at the woman nursing the infant the man remembered that he had taken the woman almost the moment she had come off the slave ship. He cursed his lust again and again. *La niña es de mi sangre. ¿Qué diablos voy a hacer con una mulata blanca?* She is of my blood. What the devil will I do with a white mulata infant? Damn it!

Some men from the Iberian peninsula had things to conceal. One man, gentle by nature, was kind and compassionate. He had managed to come to the New World even though it was forbidden by royal *cédula*. He had changed his name from López, derived from the Latin *lupus*, which others of his people expelled from Christian Spain, would translate into the languages of the countries to which they exiled themselves, Wolf, Wolk, Seiffer.

Because he would be among people of the Iberian peninsula for the rest of his life he had chosen to lie. He had adopted the Spanish names of Catholic saints to conceal his identity, but he continued to worship in secret the god of his ancestors, and his progeny in the new lands would continue to do so for hundreds of years, long after the origins of their customs would fade into oblivion.

But now, he was thinking about what it meant to be a father. When he arrived in this strange and marvelous land there had been too many days aboard ship without a woman. The ache in his loins was unbearable. No sooner had the men arrived at the village than he, like the others, had taken a native woman to his bed. The woman had been given to him.

Of these things he thought when he first contemplated the child in the arms of the mother, a young woman, a mere girl of seventeen right after she had given birth. He had taken the child from the mother with impunity, and left the mother behind.

Except to other people like himself, he looked like the Christians, which he was not. He was born in Extremadura, and he looked like many other people of the Mediterranean. He had come far away from the country of his birth, and having journeyed far away from the capital to escape the eyes of the Inquisition, he was now in the northern territory of this new land, with Luis Carvajal y de la Cueva and other people like himself. Running away from the Inquisition, in the northern lands they founded and settled el Nuevo Reino de León.

They were Sephardic Jews, and according to the Inquisition their blood was impure. *Pureza de sangre*, according to the inquisitors, meant purity of Spanish blood not contaminated by Jewish or Arabic blood. In secret he was a Jew, and now he had a wife who was also a secret Jew. He lied to her about the child. The child's mother died in childbirth, he told the woman who became his bride. He lied that the child's mother was also Jewish.

From time to time he would look at his son and see the features of the woman who had given birth to him. Sometimes the child, now seven, resembled his paternal grandfather too. There were other times when, depending on the way the boy tilted his head, the father could see in the boy's face the face of his own father. Other times he could see the face of the father of the boy's mother, a woman of this strange new land, which he and his family and his progeny would never leave. He was one of those destined never to return to the place of his birth. In two hundred years these Sephardic Jews, the colonizers of Nuevo León, would be indistinguishable from other Mexican *norteños*. Many would continue to worship in the old ways, long after the reason for doing so was lost to memory.

Fifty years and more after the great warrior people of the sun were defeated by men from the Iberian peninsula the generation of the original *conquistadores* was completely dying away. The conquest by Iberians would not have been possible without the considerable help from thousands of subjugated indigenous people who had been conquered and subjugated by the warrior people of the sun. By then, a great many Iberian men had taken native women as wives. Other Iberian men had simply mated with native women and with African slaves. Among the first generation of mestizos some were of legitimate birth. If so, they were recognized by their Iberian fathers who permitted them to dress like *gente de razón*. These *mestizos españolados* were raised to enjoy the social rights and privileges of the Spanish fathers, and if they in turn married Spanish women their offspring became "white." The progeny of mulattoes too could become "white," but only after generations of mating with people of European stock.

History books that are not well known tell secret stories that history has silenced. There are stories of vagabundos, wandering homeless men of mixed blood. Having been rejected by their Iberian fathers, by their native and African mothers, and by their families, they did not know whether they were of one race or the other. No matter what they looked like, caught between two races in a society with a rigid race, class and caste system, these tormented mestizos and mulattoes angrily and defiantly rejected the mothers and the fathers alike. Sharing the same stigma of mixed blood, history books tell us that they banded together and formed their own outcast communities:

In the woods, the mulatto strolled through the camp where they had stopped to rest and to spend the night. The anger in his green eyes was made more evident and dramatized by the frowning, wrinkled brow that emphasized two sharp, nearly vertical, lines between the eyebrows. Strolling, he brought his hands out from the side of his body, turned them over, and fixed his eyes on the back of his hands. His dark complexion was of a golden hue. Although all of his features were European, his mother's ancestry was evident in the darkness of his skin color, lightened by the father's genes, and in the texture of his chestnut hair, like that of his slave mother. His eyes took in other men like him as he passed from one slumbering man to the next. He was one of many mulattoes and mestizos, and there were men and women too who were the offspring of native women and African men.

Now, he thought, there would be more children coming into the world whose blood would combine the blood of many races—African, Indian, and Mediterranean. The features of those around him brought out a rage in his heart against the whites that had sired and abandoned them. We are homeless bastards. Our children are bastards too, he thought.

The complexions of the people in his camp ranged from very fair skin to very dark. The more he thought about belonging to this group of outcasts the more the rage mounted. The mulatto was tall and walked proudly, haughtily, angrily. He was a product of a childhood as a cast off, the son of a slave woman, despised son of a man from the Iberian Peninsula. Why do I let myself be troubled by things I cannot change? Why must I dwell endlessly on not knowing who or what I am? What race do I belong to? He dropped his hands and allowed them to swing naturally as he strolled, haughtily, with manly pride. He cursed his father and he cursed his mother and he cursed the fate that brought them together. He struggled inwardly to resist the inclination to despise himself and the others like him. ¡Chingao! We are human beings, after all.

The rage began to subside. The mulatto thought about the last raid. He and his followers had brought back several women, whites, mulatas, mestizas, Indians and Africans. His men had picked from among them. These women, he thought, will bear us many children in this God-forsaken place. The children too will grow up with the stigma of their mixed blood and dark skin. Bastard children of bastards, is that to be our legacy? From now on, we must steal and bring back white women from our raids, to lighten our children's complexion. Maybe one day our children and our grandchildren and their grandchildren can belong to the society of this land. Either that or we will have to invent our ancestors and burn books. But our children must learn to read and write first.

He thought of his intense attraction to one African woman whom they brought back from the last raid on the white community. He longed inexplicably for a woman of his African blood, but the mulatto with the green eyes had chosen a white woman to bear his children. His choice was dictated by a profound desire to whiten the race, to spare his children the curse of dark skin in a society obsessed with *pureza de sangre* and the inferiority of the castes and mixed bloods.

I marvel at the profound human biological transformation that took place during the first three hundred years when Mexico was a colony of Spain. In places, people of New Spain of the moneyed class chose to marry only people of European stock. The original vagabundos however, and their women and children, were no longer Spanish or Indian or African, not Jews or Arabs, or *godos*. Their progeny carried the blood of ancient Phoenicians, Greeks, Romans, and North Africans, of Visigoths and Arabs and Jews from the entire Mediterranean world. With the arrival of strangers who were half men—with long flowing hair on their faces—and half enormous beasts with four legs, creatures that killed with fire and thunder, all the races of the world began to converge in the new land. At first men of multiple Mediterranean ancestries began to mate with native and African women, with and without consent. Later mestizo and mulatto men and women married and had children. Then after Independence they became Mexicans all, and subsequently to Mexico came people from many other lands. To this day Mexicans continue to reconnect with their most remote origins. Nevertheless, despite a small number of people who do not accept the official history of Mexican ancestry, a true knowledge of our multiple ancestries is not well known. Such is our history.

It was a pattern in Miguel Velásquez's life that had turned him into a writer. Books of every kind, and in the recent past, books of history, always fell serendipitously into his hands.

The books fell into his hands over the years. As far back as he could remember books had inspired him to write. In countless fictional characters from novels, short stories, and plays, he had discovered compassionate and sympathetic depictions that helped him to understand aspects of his own nonconformist personality. At the same time he was struck by how much he was like the characters that represented many nations of the world.

Other books of superb scholarship had sparked his insatiable intellectual curiosity, and university teaching was the perfect means for digesting vast amounts of knowledge by presenting it to students in a systematic manner and responding to their questions and comments. As a writer and as a professor he learned that there was much to learn from students. His teaching appointment greatly stimulated his enthusiasm and quickened his interest in Mexican historiography that post-graduate work had awakened in his young manhood.

Homeless people of Berkeley had brought back the memory of walking into the Librería Madero, where he took a book down from a shelf that was filled with books about colonial Latin America and Mexico. Next to it were two books by Gonzalo Aguirre Beltrán.

Recalling his elation after buying the book, he remembered taking

ELIUD MARTÍNEZ   187 it and reading the page with the information about its publication. *Acabóse de imprimir* . . . Printed on the 21st day of November of 1957, the book was published by Editorial Jus, which later published several books about Hernán Cortés in 1984 on the occasion of the five hundredth anniversary of his birth.

The table of contents and the index told him immediately that this was a book for his personal library. Chapters II and III distinguished between Spanish Vagabonds and Mestizo and Colored Vagabonds. This book, which was to have an incremental enlightening effect on him, began with an overview of vagabonds as an historical phenomenon since ancient Roman times. In a subsequent part of the introductory chapter the author compares the vagabond way of life and its causes in England and Spain. After that the author goes into a fuller discussion of the Iberian vagabonds in New Spain, the wandering troublemakers, misfits, idlers, beggars, loafers, some of them pretenders to high social class origins—*hidalguía*—who changed their names on the ships that brought them.

In contrast to the homeless people of Berkeley and many other places that Miguel had encountered, these vagabonds were unscrupulous scoundrels from Iberia, disdainful creatures in their own country, who came wanting to rise economically on the backs of Indian and African slaves. They were hopeful of receiving *encomiendas* and becoming socially respectable *hidalgos,* sons of someone who mattered.

Disdainful of working with their hands, they mingled with beggars and sailors and pilgrims at Mediterranean and Atlantic seaports, and waited for the opportune moment to be recruited as sailors and colonists. On this side of the Atlantic they pretended they were conquistadores. In this manner Spaniards of questionable nature—the book explains—became lost among the worthy soldiers, explorers, and settlers of Spain in the Americas.

These men were a source of troubles to the Spanish Crown, because they presented a bad image of Spain and its people whose Christian God the missionary friars wanted the native population to worship. Like many of the Americans who fled England—whom Daniel Boorstin praises in one of the best books of American history—the vagabundos were an arrogant bunch, ungovernable like the Americans. It would be difficult to estimate how much the vagabundos contributed to the black legend and its antipathy to Spain.

For Miguel the most fascinating part of the book was the treatment that followed in a chapter that addressed the increasing number of discontented men who formed separate communities away from Indian and Spanish and mestizo communities. These wandering troublemakers were mestizos, in the truest sense of the word. They felt that they were not Indian or African or European.

For a writer who venerates ancestry it is fascinating to count the vagabundos among his ancestors. These mestizo and colored vagabundos in *Nueva España* formed a separate society of people, little known or studied. It is further fascinating to think of them as significant ancestors of all Mexican people. Yes, Mexico from the last quarter of the sixteenth century onward, fifty years after the Conquest, was to be a place of convergence of peoples from many parts of the world. For writers interested in their past, the most fascinating of all is the initial convergence. It was a drama of epic proportions, with lasting repercussions across centuries in the heart and spirit of the ancestors' progeny.

In the sixteenth century, Spain was faced with the immense task of populating newly acquired territories. The majority of the *conquistadores* never returned to their homeland. Some were adventurers, others were lured by legends of great wealth; some became the first explorers and immigrant settlers in the Americas. But Spain needed more people to settle and populate its territories. Spanish farmers, honorable poor people, orphans, sons from too large families, good

workmen, bricklayers, carpenters, metal workers came across the Atlantic—these good people were joined by wandering thieves, boozers,
beggars, gamblers, and other unsavory characters. It is the story of
nations.

In New Spain, Spanish vagabonds caused the Crown considerable
trouble with their pernicious activities. These idle Spanish vagrants,
when they were not assaulting and robbing travelers on the road or
Indians in their rural communities to eke out a living, would stand
outside the doors of churches and hospitals and beg. Given to vices
and disdainful of work—the extraordinary book tells us—they went
into the mines and haciendas where they started fights and caused
much trouble to workers. Acting together they robbed hardworking
Spanish farmers and cattlemen and miners. Addicted to playing cards
and dice, and betting on cockfights, the losers frequently resorted
to fights and bloodshed. Boozers who loved *aguardiente* when it was
available, they were content with *pulque* when it was not, and they
wasted away their lives is dissipation.

From the peninsula, the Crown was eager to settle its vast new territories, to promote its culture, and to convert the Indians to Christi-
anity. As Royal Protector of the Indians the Crown passed many laws
to curtail excessive activities among *encomenderos* and vagrants, often
in vain. Like some of the first Englishmen who came to the American
colonies, in New Spain too many Spanish settlers were troublemakers and difficult to govern. Eventually Spain placed Indians, Africans,
mestizos and castes in separate communities. Desirous of protecting
indigenous people the Crown decreed that they should live far from
Spaniards and mestizos, and also made provisions for the care and
welfare of the orphan children of Spaniards and mestizos—*perdidos
entre los indios*—lost among the Indians.

At this point Miguel stopped reading, closed the book, and looked
at it. He liked the format of books that were printed in Mexico. This
book was about seven by nine inches in size, a sturdy paperback,

bound in white that after many years had yellowed. The author's name, Norman F. Martin, the subtitle of the book, *Siglo XVI*; and the publisher's name and place, were in black. In larger, bold red letters, the title appeared about a third of the way from the top, in two lines, evenly spaced and centered: *Los Vagabundos en la Nueva España.*

Miguel wondered if his colleagues amply rewarded Professor Martin's valuable scholarship. The subject of the vagabundos and the so-called people of color became one of the most fascinating areas of literature and scholarship that would last to the end of his life. This book, like many others, became a source of people's stories that had not found their way into the history books. The subject was a delicate one, and controversial in Mexico. Perhaps that is why only one thousand copies of the book were published.

ABOUT THE AUTHOR

Eliud Martínez (1935-2020), artist and novelist, was the author of *Voice-Haunted Journey* (1990, U of AZ, Tempe: Bilingual Review Press) and editor of *American Identities: California Short Stories of Multiple Ancestries*. Professor Emeritus of Creative Writing and Comparative Literature at the University of California, Riverside campus, he published several scholarly articles and essays, and a book, *The Art of Mariano Azuela*. In 1975 he introduced the first multi-ethnic literature course at UC Riverside, "Chicano Literature in Comparative Ethnic Perspective." In 1985, he designed "Introduction to Race and Ethnicity," a course that became a requirement for all students at UC Riverside. In 1991, his course "Creative Writing and Ancestry" also became a required course for majors and minors in creative writing.

ABOUT INLANDIA INSTITUTE

Inlandia Institute is a regional literary non-profit and publishing house. We seek to bring focus to the richness of the literary enterprise that has existed in this region for ages. The mission of the Inlandia Institute is to recognize, support, and expand literary activity in all of its forms in Inland Southern California by publishing books and sponsoring programs that deepen people's awareness, understanding, and appreciation of this unique, complex and creatively vibrant region.

The Institute publishes books, presents free public literary and cultural programming, provides in-school and after school enrichment programs for children and youth, holds free creative writing workshops for teens and adults, and boot camp intensives. In addition, every two years, the Inlandia Institute appoints a distinguished jury panel from outside of the region to name an Inlandia Literary Laureate who serves as an ambassador for the Inlandia Institute, promoting literature, creative literacy, and community. Laureates to date include Susan Straight (2010-2012), Gayle Brandeis (2012-2014), Juan Delgado (2014-2016), Nikia Chaney (2016-2018), and Rachelle Cruz (2018-2020).

To learn more about the Inlandia Institute, please visit our website at www.InlandiaInstitute.org.

OTHER INLANDIA BOOKS